REVENGE OF THE SCIMITAR!

The front of the briefcase burst outwards soundlessly. The shot took Achmed in the chest, blowing him backwards. Rahad's second shot hit the man in the throat. The .38 pistol clattered noisily among three empty milk bottles . . .

Dropping to a crouch, Rahad reached out and patted the other man on the face. 'You really can't expect to work for two masters, Achmed. You really can't expect to get away with it.'

There was nothing else to say and Achmed could say nothing anyway. Rahad pushed the silenced barrel of his Magnum between Achmed's teeth . . .

THE PROFESSIONALS:
The Untouchables

KEN BLAKE

Based on the original screenplays by
Brian Clemens

SPHERE BOOKS LIMITED
30–32 Gray's Inn Road, London WC1X 8JL

First published in Great Britain by
Sphere Books Ltd 1982

TRADE
MARK

Set in Photon Baskerville

Printed and bound in Great Britain by
Cox & Wyman Ltd, Reading

Chapter One

The tall windows of the riverside house were open and the unpleasant smell of Thames mud, and decaying rubbish, was a powerful presence in the spacious, plushly furnished room. Air-conditioning hissed, and a light breeze ruffled the long, silken drapes on the wall. Smoke curled from a half-finished Turkish cigarette, incompletely stubbed out in a blue jade ashtray on the sideboard. But neither the smell of the smoke, nor that of the river, nor the circulation of air could disguise, in the room, the most potent stench of all: the stench of fear; the cloying odour of a man who knew his life was about to be brutally extinguished.

The man was Achmed Rajavi and he sat, now, and stared through the windows at the bright day beyond. The sound of motor-launches on the river was a pleasing distraction from the monotonous noise of the air-conditioning. The occasional noise of voices outside, some calling, some crying, some laughing, made him almost want to leave the house and run along the pathway by the river.

Almost. But not quite.

It would be pointless to run, just as it would be pointless resisting the fate that his government had designated for him. He might outwit his assassin this time; he might even kill the man first. But there would only be another, and then a third, all of them dark-suited, solemn-faced men sent calmly and coldly to gun him down. Their loss would be accountable, but unimportant. They were ciphers, expendables. But he, Achmed Rajavi, his death *meant* something. His death was important, no matter what the cost.

On the Queen Anne sideboard three photographs were arrayed and he rose, now, and went to them. The first showed his wedding, the second his beautiful young wife Saraya, the third was a portrait of his two young sons; their wide, dark eyes and smiling faces seemed almost to move as

1

they gazed out at him from the frame. His wife was almost coy in her regard, her face turned slightly, eyes a little lowered. Achmed raised the picture to his lips and kissed the cold glass above the image of her sensuous mouth. It had been months since he had last tasted the sweetness of her lips, and it would only have been two weeks more before he had found himself, again, in her passionate embrace.

Everything was ready for his return home.

Except that he had been found out, and his return home – whilst still a certainty – would be made in a box, not a jet.

He placed the photographs back on the sideboard, wiped his sweating hands on the white fabric of his robe, and walked across the room to peer out of the window at the lazy traffic on the river Thames.

About half a mile distant, driving slowly along the road parallel to the river bank, he could see a shiny black Mercedes. His stomach turned over, his heart began to pump almost frantically.

But he forced himself to be calm. He walked back to the sideboard and drew out a snub-nosed pistol, an old .38 calibre, still deadly, smuggled into England in a diplomatic bag nearly four years ago; it was a weapon he had never used in his life. He checked it now and found it loaded and ready, and after weighing it in his hand for a moment he slipped it into the pocket of a dark, suit jacket. Quickly changing his robe for the suit, and putting open-toed sandals on his feet, he waited for his killer to arrive.

The day had begun well for Tefali Rahad, and he rode in the deep, comfortable rear seat of the Mercedes with a smile on his face; behind his sunglasses there was a twinkle of pleasure in his dark eyes. As the car crawled along the road by the river, he surveyed the houses that clustered here, appreciating their variety, finding them attractive, appealing to his sense of architectural elegance.

The policeman on duty at the Embassy had saluted him today, not once, but twice. The same uniformed man had held his briefcase as he had pulled on his gloves, before driving to his appointment with Achmed Rajavi. It was these little gestures of obeisance that cheered Rahad up, made him feel smug and confident. He always liked it when he forced an Englishman into an attitude of deference. It hadn't always been that way. Years ago, when he had first come to England as a teenager, to begin his training in the art of diplomacy, all Arab persons had been treated as second class citizens, most particularly by the Security Staff laid on for them by Her Majesty's Government.

It was different now. The bobby outside the Embassy behaved just like a doorman. It was satisfying. It made Rahad despise the English even more.

He saw the house where Achmed Rajavi lived and reached a gloved hand across to tap the driver on the shoulder. 'Stop here,' he said, and the car was pulled into the kerb.

Rahad stepped out of the Mercedes, adjusted his jacket, and began to walk along the pavement, swinging his briefcase almost jauntily. He was now thirty-two years old, spare-fleshed and fit; he looked thin, and that belied his strength. He wore suits from Savile Row, and to observe him was to observe the personification of elegance. Gold cuff-links sparkled ostentatiously in the pale sunlight. His lips and bearing were touched with an arrogance learned from his friends among the British aristocracy, the younger members of which were formed into a moneyed elite that was becoming more insular, and chauvinistically resentful of the middle class, with each passing year.

Rahad trotted easily up the steps at the front of the house, not failing to notice the open windows on the second floor, and the dark, flickering shape beyond. He rang the doorbell. As he finished that simple act he glanced around at the street, and the river, and was satisfied to observe that only two launches were in eyeshot, and no pedestrians.

He was very grateful to Achmed for living in such a nice, quiet, secluded area.

Opening the briefcase he reached inside it as if shuffling among papers and turned back to the front door. The cold, heavy feel of the stock of his silenced Magnum was a pleasure to his fingers. He curled his index finger round the trigger, stroked the metal as he waited.

Distantly he heard the sound of running footsteps, ringing loud on metal: the fire escape at the back of the building, about a hundred yards away!

Ah well, no matter. There was no easy escape route for Achmed across the backs of the houses. Rahad had already established that fact.

Still wary of the open windows above, he walked easily around the building, past the tradesman's entrance, across a low fence, and then into the concreted area behind, where two garages faced him.

And a green-painted fire escape.

And the shaking, open-mouthed figure of Achmed Rajavi.

The man was still on the lower steps, peering through the rungs at the slowly approaching man. He wore a jacket over his bare skin, and his feet, clad in the open sandals, looked incongruous below the smart suit trousers. His eyes were wide, panic-filled . . . terrified.

'Hello Achmed,' said Rahad evenly, smiling broadly. 'Do you remember me?'

Achmed said nothing, but a moment later leapt the final rungs of the fire escape, landing heavily on the ground. At the same time he reached into his jacket pocket. Rahad just shook his head and grinned even wider. He allowed his target to actually produce the heavy .38 calibre and point it in his general direction before he squeezed the trigger of his concealed gun.

The front of the briefcase burst outwards soundlessly. The shot took Achmed in the chest, blowing him backwards. Rahad's second shot hit the man in the throat. The .38 pistol clattered noisily among three empty milk bottles.

Achmed half lay, half sat on the ground, blood on his chest and running from the sleeve of his jacket where he tried to prop himself up on the ground.

Rahad walked slowly across to him, drawing his silenced gun from the useless briefcase. Achmed watched him, eyes half-narrowed, flickering. Dropping to a crouch, Rahad reached out and patted the other man on the face. 'You really can't expect to work for two masters, Achmed. You really can't expect to get away with it.'

There was nothing else to say, and Achmed could say nothing anyway. Rahad pushed the silenced barrel of his Magnum between Achmed's teeth.

With a quick smile he squeezed the trigger. The expression in Achmed's eyes never changed.

Sir John Terringham watched silently as his attractive, brunette secretary entered the office and seemed almost to glide towards him across the thick-piled carpet. She picked up his empty bone-china tea cup and deposited, in its place, a thin sheaf of papers. Terringham glanced at them and nodded.

'Will there be anything else, sir?' the girl asked, and Terringham smiled and said, 'No thank you, Miss Atkinson.'

She turned and walked from the expansive suite that was Terringham's office, glancing pleasantly at the gruff, grizzled man who sat relaxedly in a deep, leather armchair, near to the window.

When she had gone, Terringham pushed the papers to one side and reached into an oak box for a fat, Cuban cigar.

'Havana, George?'

'Not just now, thanks all the same,' said George Cowley, turning away from the Foreign Office official to peer out into the bright day. Terringham lit up and puffed contentedly for a moment. He was in his sixties; he had deep, narrow eyes and was well groomed, well dressed; he had the look about him of a man who found smiling easy, and who could smile to cover his total ruthlessness. On his desk in front of him was only one single personal effect, a small photograph of his wife, Alison, and his daughter Clare.

'We must face facts, George. We have a problem.' Terringham paused for a moment and peered at the smoking tip of his cigar. 'The Embassy protects its cultural attachés quite formidably. We've dealt with them in the past.'

'Cultural attaché!' snapped Cowley. 'Official bloody murderer!' Angrily he rose to his feet and walked across to Terringham's desk, hands thrust into the pockets of his pin-striped trousers. His cold gaze rested, for a moment, on the Ministry man's hard eyes. They had been acquaintances for many years – Cowley would not have used the word friend – having worked together in MI5, and later on combined operations between MI5 and CI5. Terringham had great

5

respect for Cowley's tough way of dealing with the delicate and dangerous assignments that he and his team were required to handle. Cowley had slightly less respect for the desk-bound official, but Terringham was one of the most co-operative of the men from the Foreign Office, and was a useful contact, if not capable of cynical manipulation.

Terringham suddenly smiled, though it was a gloomy smile, accompanied by a shrug of his broad shoulders. 'Official murderer? We have no proof of that, George. Absolutely no proof. Not even from Special Branch.'

Cowley was exasperated. His northern accent became more pronounced when he was angry, and a thin line of sweat appeared below his hairline. 'Och, come *on*, Sir John. Proof? It *had* to be Rahad. It was his style, his style completely. Vicious, cold, complete. *And* the copper on duty at the Embassy remembers him leaving just about the time of the killing, with a briefcase that he didn't bring back!'

Terringham banged the table, firmly, pointedly, reaching with his other hand to place the cigar in the built-in desk ashtray. 'I've seen the reports, George,' he said irritably, 'And I agree with you. Undoubtedly it was Tefali Rahad, *but* . . .' Cowley tried to say something, but Terringham's raised voice cut him short, 'But we have no proof.' He leaned back.

'You need proof to expel him from the country?' Cowley was back at the window, disconsolate, staring out across Whitehall.

'We need something. We need something pinned on him, some trivial breach of the law that we can prove. Otherwise, the official view is why disturb the cordial relations between his country and ours?'

'Aye,' growled George Cowley, with a cynical little smile on his lips. 'And in the meantime he'll go on killing. What is it they say? "Engaged in the execution of enemies of the State". Cold blooded bloody murder by any other name . . .'

Before Terringham could comment his desk buzzer sounded, and when he flicked it on a brisk male voice reported that, 'Mister Tefali Rahad to see you Sir John . . .'

'What?' breathed Cowley in astonishment, staring hard at Sir John Terringham, who merely made a tiny movement of his head as if to say, 'I've no idea what he's doing here.'

'He insists on seeing you, sir,' said the voice from the desk. 'He knows he has no appointment, but insists that he comes on a matter of great urgency.'

'Then show him in,' said Terringham, and as he leaned back in his chair his face took on an expression of total blankness, but with eyes narrowed, searching. Cowley looked towards the door, murmuring, 'Not possible, I suppose, that he's come to give himself up . . .'

'Hardly . . .'

The door to the suite opened with such abruptness that it seemed to Cowley that someone had kicked it. Sir John Terringham rose to his feet as the elegantly dressed and arrogant form of Tefali Rahad walked swiftly across the carpet, briefcase in one hand, the other thrust into his trouser pocket.

'Mister Rahad . . .' said Terringham, and the Arab briefly, almost angrily, shook the man's hand.

Cowley stared hard at the killer. He looked so ordinary in one way, a dusky, handsome sort of man, steel-eyed gaze, self assured, humourless, the sort of businessman that could be seen from Scotland to Tangiers; in one way unremarkable. And yet there was an aura about Rahad, an almost tangible essence of perversion; to Cowley it seemed nothing less than that he could *smell* the murder on the man's hands.

'Sir John,' Rahad said briskly, almost stating the name. 'I'm sorry I had to insist on seeing you, but it is of great urgency, I couldn't wait . . .'

Cutting him off in mid-flow, Terringham waved a hand towards Cowley, who inwardly smiled at Terringham's cool. 'This is George Cowley, Mister Rahad.'

Cowley acknowledged Rahad with the briefest of nods as the Arab's gaze centred on him. Rahad seemed uninterested in him, almost impatient, but said aloud, 'Mister Cowley. I have heard of you.' His dark eyes gleamed, his full lips moistened, his gaze flickered up and down Cowley's figure. Cowley was being assessed, documented, filed. Rahad said, trying to be insulting, 'You are much smaller than I imagined.'

That provoked a chuckle from Cowley, more for its obviousness than for its content. 'So was Henry the Eighth,' he said, and the point was not lost on the cultural attaché. Cowley began to walk to where his coat lay across the armchair. 'I'll be off, Sir John. Leave you to it.'

But Rahad said loudly, 'No! No, please stay, Mister Cowley. This may concern you.' He turned back to Terringham and leaned forward on the desk. 'I wish to register the strongest complaint.'

Quite unmoved by Rahad's hostility, Terringham asked quietly, 'Complaint about what, precisely?'

'The fact that I am being followed,' shouted Rahad, clearly angry that Terringham was playing so unflappably coy.

'I assure you, Mister Rahad . . .'

Rahad straightened and shook his head vigorously, interrupting Terringham with, 'No, do not bother to deny it . . . I know about these things . . .'

'I wasn't about to deny anything,' said Terringham, evenly. Cowley stepped forward and said, 'Of course, as *cultural attaché* you'd naturally be protected . . .' he emphasised the words 'cultural attaché', attempting to inject just sufficient of a note of sarcasm into his voice that Rahad would bristle.

But Rahad merely looked at him, smiled thinly and said, '*Much* smaller.' He again looked Terringham square in the eye and went on, 'You will, of course, take all steps to remedy this situation? We shall regard this as an *informal* complaint . . . hopefully there will be no need to register a formal one?' He picked up his briefcase and turned abruptly on his heel, walking away from the desk as he said, 'Thank you for your time Sir John. Mister Cowley.'

As the door closed behind Rahad, Cowley chuckled, shook his head and came to sit on the edge of Terringham's desk.

Terringham was not as cool, now, as when Rahad had been confronting him, and he said almost furiously, 'The gall of the bloody man!'

'He must have seen the Special Branch tail. It still didn't stop him killing, but it must be cramping his style.'

Terringham leaned forward, cradling his head in his hands, staring thoughtfully at the closed door. 'We've got to

8

do something about him, George. It's too hot for the Home Office to handle. I'm afraid CI5 must take a hand. Your line of work, I imagine.'

Cowley grinned. 'Right up our street, Sir John. In fact I've been giving the matter not a little thought; the matter of how to fix our Tefali Rahad. I've got a couple of lads who can play their roles perfectly. All I need is a beautiful young woman, with a classy background.'

He picked up the photograph of Alison and Clare Terringham, stared at it thoughtfully, then at Terringham himself, who was looking distinctly concerned.

'You don't mean Clare . . .'

'Aye, I *do* mean Clare. Don't worry, Sir John. I only want to borrow your daughter. My lads will take exceptional care of her.'

Sprawled in one of the deep armchairs of Bodie's small but elegantly furnished flat, Ray Doyle looked weatherbeaten, scruffy and fed up. His tousled fair hair was in wild disarray, his eyes sleep-rimmed and dark, his full lips almost pouted with irritation as his gaze flickered here and there about the tasteful, unobtrusive decoration of his partner's abode. His feet were up on a coffee table, crossed at the ankle, and his hands were thrust into the pockets of his faded jeans; after a thirty-six hour stake-out, alone, he looked settled for an evening of sullen silence.

By contrast, Bodie was decked out in impeccable style, a dark evening suit, tailored and fashionable, lace shirt opened at the neck, exposing an expanse of tanned chest, set off by a small gold medallion. He was shaved, groomed, smooth and handsome and, as he stared at himself in a mirror there was a definite smirk on his face; every so often he would glance at Doyle and wink, then chuckle, then whistle happily to himself as he surveyed his features in the reflection.

'Dog,' said Doyle irritably.

'Handsome dog,' corrected Bodie.

'You're so vain sometimes it makes me sick.'

Bodie smiled, turned to face his truculent partner; his dark eyes flashed with humour. 'It's the details that win hearts. This is a double assignment . . . one for Cowley, and one *strictly* personal.'

'She'll laugh in your face.'

Bodie turned back to the mirror, shook his hips. 'I'll turn the other cheek.'

'She'll think you're jumped up.' Doyle was determined not to give an inch. But Bodie countered, 'She'll get a new meaning of the word "jump".'

Deflated by Bodie's glowing confidence, Doyle scowled again. 'Terringham's daughter! What a score. And I was on nights . . .'

Bodie placed a wallet in the inside pocket of his jacket, and fitted a white handkerchief into the left breast pocket, just a touch of a corner showing. He watched Doyle for a second and said, 'Ring up a girl or two. You can use this place. Ring up that redhead, Chrissie whatsername . . .'

'Pearson? She's into Buddhists.'

'Well, that blonde then. Sue Barker. Touch of class . . .'

'Likes rugby players.'

Bodie sighed. He'd done his best. 'There's a can of lager in the fridge. Have fun.'

'Terringham's daughter . . .' muttered Doyle, taking his feet off the table and standing up.

'Good things always come to the deserving,' said Bodie, rubbing it in. He inspected himself one last time in the mirror, 'And the aristocracy deserve me . . . lucky girl . . . lucky, lucky girl. . . .'

Doyle looked like a man about to throw up. He said, though, 'If her father's a "Sir", does that make her an "Honourable" . . . or a "lady"? Or what?'

Bodie looked over his shoulder and winked. 'A dame. And I know about dames.'

The door buzzer sounded and both men reacted, almost startled. 'That'll be her now,' gloated Bodie. 'Come to whisk me away in her limousine by Mister Rolls and Mister Royce. . . .'

He crossed to the door. Doyle muttered, 'She'll see through you in an instant. Boy doing man's job.' Bodie opened the door with theatrical emphasis, bowing slightly to admit the girl who stood on the other side. He immediately straightened as he caught sight of her, and Doyle's chagrin peaked as Clare Terringham stepped into the room.

She looked a little older than her nineteen tender years; she was tall, elegantly slim, but full breasted, a fact immediately obvious through the thin, open-necked blouse she wore. Wide-eyed and unsmiling, she shook back perfectly cut brown hair, and surveyed each of the two CI5 men in turn.

Looking at Bodie, then, she said, 'I think you should know from the start that I'm unofficially engaged.'

Bodie gave a little bow, then grinned, holding out his arm for Clare Terringham to take. 'I shall try to respect that, Clare. I shall try very hard.' He looked at Doyle. 'Goodnight Raymond.'

But as they stepped to the door, Clare Terringham said quite loudly, 'I also should tell you that I don't really go for older men.'

Bodie quickly closed the door to drown out the sound of Doyle's raucous, mocking laughter.

Clare's limousine was indeed a Rolls Royce, and it was waiting for them outside, purring softly. Bodie followed the girl into the back seat, and noticed, with some humour, that she huddled into the corner, as far from him as possible.

The car slid away from the kerb, heading for Kensington.

After a few minutes of silence, Clare staring hard out of the window, Bodie staring at Clare, he slid closer to the girl. Clare Terringham reacted immediately, almost with shock, certainly with a little irritation.

'This has got to *look* right,' said Bodie.

'I told you, I'm unofficially engaged.'

'It's just like acting out a role, Clare. Nothing to it if you relax and think yourself into the part.' He smiled, trying to be reassuring, and reached for her hand. The hand was jerked away. By the glaring lights of London she looked startlingly attractive, her profile sharp, mature, handsome. And solemn.

'I'm not an actress,' she said pointedly.

'Well, I'll lead,' Bodie suggested, putting his arm around her shoulders, 'And you just follow. Do as I do . . .'

'Certainly not!' She pulled free of his partial embrace, and

11

tried to stare out of the window again.

Bodie, with a great deal of reasonableness in his voice, said, 'I don't see what difference it makes. I'm married . . .'

Clare Terringham looked round at him, puzzled. 'Are you?'

'To my work,' Bodie made clear and smiled. 'The things I have to go through . . .' And this time, as he pulled her close into an appearance of the loving couple, she stayed where she was, stiff, unhappy, but unobjecting.

In no time at all, it seemed to Bodie, the chauffeur had slid the Rolls to a stop outside the brilliantly lit frontage of the *Casino d'Or*. This was a busy area at night, sightseers, late-night shoppers, tourists seeking some of the best food in London. As Bodie stepped from the car he was aware of the eyes upon him; mostly the envious glances of the mundane crowds, he was unnervingly aware of the unobtrusive observation of two men who stood near to the casino entrance. He noticed them, but didn't allow them to notice him taking account of their surveillance. He had seen them in the casino before and knew that they were 'sucker touts'.

Bodie was a sucker, and he hoped they'd detected that.

He leaned back into the Rolls Royce to kiss Clare on the lips; she turned her face at the last minute, and his kiss landed on her cheek. But before she could move across the seat out of his grasp, Bodie reached into the car and took Clare Terringham firmly by the shoulders, pulling her body to his and kissing her full and hard on the mouth.

She looked flustered; her eyes had widened and she stared at Bodie, but there was no objection, no resentment. Just surprise. And just a hint of warmth.

'An important lesson, kiddiwink,' Bodie patronised softly, 'With age comes experience.'

The car drove off.

Bodie turned and stepped towards the *Casino d'Or*.

Despite its garish exterior, the inside of the casino was a dimly lit, dingy dump. It had a large bar, attended by two waistcoated, but sullen, barmen; it had a scattering of tables, some set up for cards, some for roulette; it had a small stage on which two tired looking girls, wearing skimpy costumes

12

that appeared to be as fatigued as their listless owners, danced through a routine to soft music. There was activity at the tables, there was a clattering of glass, and the murmur of voices; little enjoyment, by the sound of it. The club would not have been out of place in Soho; at this junction between Kensington and Notting Hill Gate it was quite incongruous. Hence the sparse attendance and the querulous, almost embarrassed response to its presence on the street by the night-active population of the area.

The owner of this dive was a tall, muscular black who had been known merely as Nero for so long that there were times when even he couldn't remember his real name. He was forty years old, scarred, cunning and perilously close to being a dead-beat. He had opened this club four years back, with money from the local Manor, and only his willing and energetic co-operation with the organised crime of this part of London kept him in business. Profitwise, the *Casino d'Or* was a disaster.

Nero had been born a Liverpool street urchin, had knifed his first man at the age of eleven, and had soon become part of the organised street crime of that decaying city. He had come south as a bodyguard, and in ten years had made London his home; he had earned sufficient respect in the big city to eventually go independent. But he was in no doubt that his usefulness was limited to the number of 'easy takes' that he could set up for his master. Mugs. Suckers. Rich boys, or hard boys, who could be taken for a ride, and then bent to certain uses.

He had one in mind right now and had sent to Johnny Hollis to let the man know that he was on the track of a likely lad.

Hollis's street man was a squat, repugnant East-ender called Hart. Hart was red-faced and sweated a lot, but he had a punch like a pile-driver. Nero had felt that fist just once, and once was enough.

Hart arrived at the casino looking hot and irritable. He mopped his face with a black handkerchief, watched the listless dancing for a moment and curled his lips in distaste.

'Why the hell d'you keep them two on?'

Nero grinned. 'I pay 'em with . . .' he trailed off, raised his arm, fist clenched. 'They're okay. Too much sex and the punters get distracted.'

Hart changed the subject to matters at hand. 'You called Mister Hollis.'

'He told me to keep my eyes open for a new mug. I always do what Mister Hollis says.'

Hart shook his head, glancing away from the black. 'You found a target? Where is he?'

'He'll be here. And I dunno if he's a real target. But I think so. Been in here two nights in a row, wins some, loses some. He talks big, but I ain't sure. I'm kind of cultivating him. There he is now ...' Nero nodded towards the entrance, and Hart followed his glance.

Bodie stepped down the short stairs, smiling at the girl who came to take his coat.

Hart frowned. 'Looks heavy. Looks hard.'

Nero said, 'Looks is nothing. This boy's a sucker. Gets real upset when he loses. Drinks a lot. Brags that he's screwing some deb. We ain't proved that yet.'

'I'll take your word for it,' said Hart, looking up at the black. 'Stay with him, Nero. If he's worth cultivating ... well, we'll be glad to help you with the harvest.'

As Hart strolled discreetly away, Nero sauntered up to Bodie and smiled in greeting. 'Can't stay away, eh?'

Bodie waved a clenched fist, grinning as he did so. 'Feel *lucky* tonight, Nero. Feel *hot*. Those cards are going to run for me, you wait and see.'

'Nice to see a man with confidence. You want a drink?'

Bodie nodded. 'Double scotch. Ice.'

The barman had heard the order and at Nero's glance went away to fix the drink. Nero lounged on the bar. 'You come prepared, like all the best Boy Scouts?'

Bodie reached for his wallet, drew out the thick wad of ten pound notes. 'This prepared enough, Nero?' He accepted his drink, sipped it, smacked his lips.

Nero watched him with a half smile on his face. 'If you're ready, then, the boys're waiting in the back room. Nice and quiet.'

'Lead on,' said Bodie, and didn't fail to notice Nero's quick glance across the room to the short, flushed man who

14

stood close to the stage watching.

Bodie assessed the man quickly, pretending, as he did so, that he was watching the gormless dancers.

It galled Bodie to lose at cards.

He loved poker, especially stud, although in English clubs draw poker seemed to be the most favoured variation, and he had become a cool, smart and successful player of the game.

Why, only last week he'd taken Ray Doyle for a fiver, after a marathon two hour game.

Tonight he lost over a grand at the table, having at one point racked up three wins, and doubled his money. The cards ran very well with him, and it infuriated him to discard half of a pair of Kings, or go for a pair instead of the full house that he just *knew* he could make.

But rules were rules, and a plan of action was a plan of action; and Bodie had to lose at cards, and take the scorn, and go back and take it all again.

At four in the morning he was cleaned out. Nero met him outside the back room where the *real* games were played, and in the black's eyes there was something that seemed, to Bodie, to be of a mocking nature. Defiantly, Bodie said, 'Okay, you win some, you lose some.'

Nero chuckled. 'I heard of cards running, man, but never *away* from you. You sure got taken.'

'I'll be back,' said Bodie, and Nero shrugged.

'Any time, man. Any time. Can fix you up with a game anytime you like. Just call.'

Bodie moved towards the phone in the corner. 'At least I don't have to walk home.'

Aware that he was being watched, Bodie stepped out into the street; it was cool, deserted, rather desolate. He huddled inside his coat until he saw Clare Terringham's Rolls approaching, and when it stopped for him he practically jumped into the back.

Clare was waiting for him, and she glanced out the window at the two men who lounged against the wall, watching the car depart. She ought to have been tired, but she seemed fresh, very much awake. Bodie could detect the

15

subtle hint of an expensive perfume.

And she had changed her clothes too; she looked much sleeker, much sexier.

'Was it successful?' she asked, and added, 'Did you get what you wanted in there?'

Bodie stared at the girl, then smiled thinly. 'I got what I wanted in the club. Yes. But then I always get what I want.'

'I'm sure you do.'

'Something different about you, Clare.'

Clare Terringham shrugged, looked down at herself. 'Oh yes, I . . . er . . . I had to change. I spilt some wine on my frock earlier in the evening.'

Bodie shook his head. 'Wasn't just your dress that got changed. Your attitude has changed too. It's softer. I like it.'

Clare looked at him, then looked away. Bodie took her hand very lightly and the girl's eyes lowered; her other hand covered Bodie's and she slid a little closer to the man.

Bodie leaned forward and rapped on the glass between front and back seats. 'Jeeves. Take the long way home.'

Chapter Two

To snare such a wily old fox as Tefali Rahad, a very cunning trap was needed. Cowley was laying that trap with care, confidence and a great deal of thought. Each move in the sequence of events that would lead to the ensnarement was rehearsed in his mind repeatedly, worked out against the setting of the whole *danse macabre*. He had rarely devised so complex a game for Doyle and Bodie to play.

Complicated games are dangerous; they go wrong easily.

That's why Cowley took his time, why he directed his men with all the thoughtful concern of a film director schooling his players.

Bodie had started his act. Now it was Ray Doyle's turn to go into action.

At night, in a wide, quiet street that would soon be bustling with a demonstration against Government policy, Doyle met with Cowley, and a lean, pale-faced but hard-looking copper called Martin Fisk.

Doyle and Fisk sized each other up, shook hands firmly, grinned, recognised the danger potential in each other, and relaxed.

Cowley, face impassive in the darkness, spread out three photographs on top of his car and shone a bright torch upon them. 'This is Harry Taylor. Take a good, hard look. Memorise the face. Take a look at Doyle. Memorise *his* face.'

Fisk studied photograph and CI5 man, then passed the photograph back to Cowley. 'And you want this Taylor nicked, is it? You want him picked up?'

'In a manner of speaking . . .' said Doyle.

'Obstruction, loitering . . . breathing too hard in a public place? You name it, he gets picked up for it.'

Doyle hefted a workman's bag onto Cowley's highly polished car roof; grinned as Cowley grimaced; the bag had hit the car with a clatter of metal tools. Turning to Fisk,

17

Doyle said, 'A little bag of tools, and a man's natural curiosity. It's all you'll need. Except, that is,' Doyle raised a fist, cradled it gently in his other hand, 'Except for a little play-acting.'

Cowley took his leave, and Fisk and Doyle climbed into the CI5 pool car that Doyle had drawn, and drove slowly to the rendezvous point with Harry Taylor.

Taylor's movements were well known, by now, and at two in the morning he would head back to his digs across the railway bridge over Portland Street. The site was dim, shadowy and rather menacing, and Fisk, in his uniform, added to that menace as he patrolled up and down the street, waiting for Doyle's signal to get into hiding.

Taylor, with wonderful predictability, appeared on the bridge at almost exactly the hour Doyle had hoped. He was a young man, studious looking, with the thin round-the-chin beard that had once characterised Quakers, and now was more familiarly linked with Marxists. He was dressed in casual jeans and leather jacket, and he walked briskly through the darkness, long hair bouncing about his shoulders.

As he stepped into Portland Street he tripped over the dark leather valise, the tools clattering as he inadvertently kicked it into the gutter.

He reached down and picked the case up, then squatted on the pavement and opened the bag. Reaching inside he pulled out a peculiarly shaped tool, neither screwdriver nor spanner, an odd and oddly functionless piece of equipment. Puzzled he reached into the bag again . . .

Then yelled with surprise and shock as a hand grabbed him on the shoulder and yanked him upright.

It took Taylor a brief moment to notice that his assailant was a policeman. Fisk held him for a moment, then let him go, but pushed him until Taylor was up against the wall of the viaduct.

'Face the wall,' said Fisk. 'Quickly. Face the wall.'

'Why are you doing this?' said Taylor, aggrieved and angry. 'I'm on my way home, that's all.'

'With a neat little case of housebreaking tools. Very likely, sir. Very likely indeed.'

Taylor tried to turn round, saying, 'They're not mine.'

Fisk slammed him back against the wall, punched him lightly in the left kidney and snapped, 'Stay put.'

Face against the wall, Taylor almost whined. 'Listen, I just tripped over the bag. They were lying in the street, and I tripped over them.'

'Tell it to the sergeant,' said Fisk, picking up the bag, then placing a firm hand on Taylor's shoulder. 'Come on lad. Let's get going.'

Taylor struggled in the policeman's grasp, trying to pull away. 'You're not taking me in . . !'

As Fisk grappled Taylor to the ground a figure came running out of the shadows. Taylor heard the sound of a dull thud, felt Fisk's grip on him relax. A second thud, and the policeman gasped, collapsed to the ground on his knees, then fell forward onto the pavement.

The curly haired man who stood there, breathing hard, looking wild, shouted, 'C'mon! Quick!'

Taylor jumped to his feet and started to run. He noticed the other man grab the valise of tools and follow.

He didn't notice the grim little smile on Fisk's face as, through half opened eyes, he watched Doyle and Taylor making ground into the night.

'I owe you. I'm grateful.'

Doyle was driving. The car sped through the London streets, imprudently fast, yet satisfyingly so. Doyle was grim-faced, concentrating on the job at hand. Taylor watched him, querulous, perturbed.

When his rescuer said nothing, Taylor prompted, 'Why'd you help me?'

'Fuzz!' said Doyle spitefully. He glanced at his passenger and grinned. 'When I see fuzz pushing someone around my blood boils. Know what I mean?'

Taylor stared at the road ahead. 'I know exactly what you mean.'

'Besides,' added Doyle, 'they *were* my tools.'

Taylor directed them to his own premises, not his flat but the headquarters of his 'movement'. He seemed reluctant to talk about exactly what it was he represented, he and the rest of his youth organisation. But Doyle played the situation like he was glad of somewhere just to cool his heels and unwind.

The room that Taylor took him to was small, scruffy and very very dingy. It was set up mainly as a printing room, the rusting, cumbersome-looking press occupying almost a third of the space. Pamphlets, books, leaflets and screwed up balls of paper littered the floor and every available surface. The walls were covered with posters, photographs, cuttings and cartoons. Doyle picked out one poster in particular. It showed a fair headed girl, quite plain, wearing spectacles, presented as Anna Jones. Doyle studied the face for several moments, noticing the intensity in the girl's eyes, the ruthless curve of her lips. She was not pretty, but she was quite remarkable.

Taylor fetched two small cans of beer from the tiny fridge in the room. Doyle gratefully swigged his, whilst Taylor just sipped.

Doyle asked, 'What's all this, then? Political?'

But Taylor avoided answering the question directly. 'For a bloke like you,' he said, placing his can down on a table, 'the word is therapeutical.'

'Don't get you.'

'A chance every so often to bash the fuzz ... and all in a good cause. I'm serious. We can always use a bit of extra muscle.'

Doyle drained his can, and stared hard at the younger man. Taylor's eyes were burning with an intensity that Doyle rarely saw. The man was a fanatic, that much was obvious. And he wanted to recruit Ray Doyle ... to the service of bashing policemen! Doyle would have happily thrashed this little bastard around the room, but he had to act, and he acted out a delighted smile.

'I like the sound of it ... but I'm not sure. I'll think about it.'

Taylor homed in. 'Come on Ray. I could join you up right now ... a fiver for the year.' He grinned. 'That's something else we can always do with – money.'

Late morning, in the *Casino d'Or*, Nero was racking up bottles behind the bar, checking to make sure that the full array of drinks was available for the long night to come.

Bodie walked in, dressed up to the nines, looking smooth, suave, and confident.

'Well, well,' said Nero, leaning down on the bar and looking Bodie up and down. 'The lamb returns to the slaughter house. Good mornin' to you.'

'I'm no lamb,' said Bodie, feigning a touch of truculence. 'Just had a run of bad luck, that's all.'

Nero hooted with laughter, genuinely felt. 'A *run*? Man, that was no run, that was a *mara*-thon!'

Bodie just smiled. He sat at the bar and unfurled a roll of notes, all tens and twenties, amounting to nearly one thousand pounds sterling. Nero looked at the money, then up at the man. His black face creased in a frown.

'You're early, man. I ain't been to bed yet.'

'I said I'd be back, Nero.'

'Yeah, but . . . come on, man. *This* time of day?'

Bodie wagged a finger. 'Maybe you forgot what you told me. I can find a game anytime, you said. Anytime at all. That's what you said. Well that's fine with me. Here I am. Set me up with a game.'

Nero took a deep breath, eyes wide with disbelief (at his own good fortune, no doubt!). He filled a tall glass with scotch and ice and set it down in front of Bodie, who picked it up, stared at it, drank.

'It's on the house,' said Nero.

'Glad to hear it.'

Nero shook his head, fixing Bodie with his dark-eyed stare. 'I always admire a man who don't know when he's been good and proper beat . . . '

'Who says I'm beat?'

'But man, you *are*. Three times you've dropped a bundle in this place, cleaned out three times in a row. And still you come back.' Nero frowned. 'If that wasn't so enticing, why, that'd be downright suspicious! You're either some freak millionaire getting his kicks out of watching the expressions of joy on a winning man's face, or you're so dumb you don't know when to lie down and die.'

'Just fix the game, Nero.'

Bodie drank his scotch and watched the puzzled black.

Nero straightened up and glanced at the phone. He was thinking hard, and Bodie's intuitive streak told him that *some* explanation of his repeatedly coming back for more punishment was needed.

He was clearly not a millionaire; and Nero would have known by now that he wasn't *that* stupid. Act all he might, it wasn't possible for Bodie to disguise that streak of hard that ran through him like quartz in soft rock.

Nero cocked his head as he stared at the CI5 man. 'Why you *really* keep coming back? Just revenge? Just feel lucky?'

Bodie drained his glass, tapped it on the counter and Nero, hesitating only briefly, sloshed a good belt of whisky over the melting cubes of ice. 'I came here last night and dropped a grand. That makes three grand in all that your card sharps have had off me . . . '

'They ain't sharps, man. That game's straight.'

Bodie waved him silent. 'Straight, crooked, or just a little biased, no one takes me four times in a row! I felt bad last night, Nero, but I've been out to raise funds, and I intend to take back all that I've lost. Now I have to tell you,' he leaned across the bar, staring the black so hard in the eyes that Nero began to feel uncomfortable. 'I have to tell you that I'm feeling frustrated. Either I get back into a game, or I start hitting someone. And you're the only person here, Nero.'

The black smiled. 'Okay, okay. No sooner said than done.' He walked towards the phone, looking back at the smiling Bodie and jibing, 'Old Nero can always find someone to take your money. Old Nero always glad to oblige.'

Tefali Rahad's suite in the Embassy was on the top floor, and was so spacious that it included rooms on both front and back of the building. For a cultural attaché it was a ridiculously extravagant set of rooms to have had allocated to him; but Rahad had power in the Embassy, and with his home government.

What Tefali Rahad wanted, Tefali Rahad was given. Because Rahad could offer something quite invaluable, something preserving in an aspic of pleasure, luxury and privilege.

He was the Hand of Vengeance, the cold finger of anger on an arm that stretched from the Middle East to Western Europe. He was The Man, and those in real power back in his homeland knew just how valuable was his strength to them, and acknowledged that to keep that strength working for them they had to cater to his needs, to his whims, to his varied tastes . . .

One of his tastes was for western women of a particular type: tall and built well, with blonde hair in great, curled masses on their heads, and tiny, fine down upon the rest of their bodies. If it had been pointed out to Rahad that he was reacting against the stereotype of the Eastern beauty, with her shorter height, smaller figure, and dark features, Rahad might have nodded with interest, and then laughed.

He didn't care *why* he liked blondes; he just knew it as a fact, and was never without the company of a woman who conformed to his taste.

And he *never* paid of necessity, although he was generous with his 'tips'.

Rahad had a voracious sexual appetite and occupied large numbers of hours in the satiation of that hunger; in a way this calmed him for the performance of his work, each 'project' of which might only take a matter of an hour from leaving the Embassy to returning, but which drained him emotionally, and which could set up disturbing currents in his mind. Rahad was not a mindless, cold-blooded killer. His intelligence and imagination would not allow him the luxury of ignoring the assassination that he was to achieve. He would think it through in great detail, planning for every eventuality, trying to imagine every detail that might go wrong . . . even to the unexpected attack on him by his intended victim.

It had upset him greatly that Achmed Rajavi had been waiting for him, gun in hand. How had Achmed *known*? Quite evidently his security was not water-tight, and it was equally evident to him that the Home Office, and almost certainly CI5, were aware of him, and suspicious of him.

All of which was capable of making him anxious, although he was too confident to imagine that some impenetrable net of Law and Order was closing in on him.

He would simply lay low for a while, function as a normal cultural attaché, and refuse all 'projects' for six months.

Anxiety, tension, these were the occupational hazards of the intelligent killer; sexual encounters of the uninhibited kind were the soothing balm.

Naked, Rahad sprawled on his settee two days after the Achmed killing, watching the nude girl before him with an almost academic interest, now. He was drenched with sweat, and the aroma of intercourse was heavy on him. He smoked a short cheroot and picked at his nose; there were no words that he wished to say to the girl. His excitement when she had arrived, and slowly disrobed, had induced in him a poetic, romantic flurry that had brought a blush to her cheeks, and caused her to moan her love during the long afternoon of Rahad's vigorous possession. Spent, exhausted, numb, he hoped she would go as soon as possible. But Rahad didn't believe in discourtesy.

As he watched her pull her flimsy underclothes onto her body, he thought wryly of how this weakness for women would be a fatal weakness in a man who could not control his passions. His awareness of the power in his body and his mind was Tefali Rahad's greatest turn-on. Even greater than eighteen-year-old blondes who could have made Jayne Mansfield look like an underdeveloped school-girl.

When she was dressed, the girl – Rahad thought her name was Linda Karr, and he would ask for her again – came across to him and crouched between his spread legs. She reached to touch him one last time, but Rahad slapped her hand away with an irritable gesture.

Slightly sulkily the girl asked, 'Will I see you again?'

Rahad shrugged. 'Possibly. I'll call you if and when I need you.'

'I'd like to see you again. I enjoyed you, Tefali.'

'That is of no interest to me at all.'

Getting the message of his coldness, the girl stood. 'Was I. worth a . . . *tip*?' she asked, a hard edge to her voice.

Rahad indicated a purse on the coffee table. 'Take it all. And get out.'

The on-duty policeman outside the Embassy saluted the girl as she came tripping lightly down the steps. She smiled at him, but was conscious of his eyes on her as she walked the few paces to where her sports car was parked, and bent to get inside.

She felt angry, frustrated; she hated Rahad, and yet she very much wanted to go back. Both anger and hate were evident in the way she streaked away from the kerb, nearly colliding with a passing taxi, and accelerated towards Gloucester Road.

In the mirror she noticed the green Capri that was behind her, and she might have seen that it had pulled out from about a hundred yards away at the exact moment her own car had started up. But that fact had escaped her, and she took no more than an academic interest in the vehicle behind her. She continued to speed.

At the lights at Cromwell Road she swore irritably as she was forced to stop. If the car in front of her had just gone slightly quicker she too could have got through on amber. She sat behind the wheel, tapping her fingers impatiently, waiting for the red light to change to green.

There was a knock on her window. She was startled to see a young man, with curly brown hair and an impish grin, peering in at her.

'Open up darlin'' he shouted, and tapped the window again.

Confused, bemused, she leaned over and wound the window down. 'What the hell do *you* want?'

Ray Doyle leaned into the sports car. The lights turned green, and the car behind began to sound its horn, but with the man's head inside the vehicle she couldn't drive off.

'Fancy a nice time, darling?'

'Bugger off!'

Doyle flipped open his ID case and thrust it towards her face, looking rueful as he added, 'On the other hand, it could be quite a bad time.'

The girl stared at the ID, then at Doyle, then sank back in her seat, gasping with exasperation.

Ray Doyle's apartment was considerably untidier than Bodie's, furniture, magazines and clothes scattered chaotically about the place, only a small shelf of trophies standing orderly in one corner of the room. Cowley would have used the word dishevelled to describe the flat, and in this way, apartment mimicked owner.

Cowley sat, now, nursing a rather good malt whisky in a brandy glass (Doyle had managed to smash his two whisky glasses in a frolicsome night two evenings ago). Ray Doyle himself was making coffee in the small kitchen. He was still tired, and wasn't sure whether his body was in breakfast time or dinner time.

He just knew he was hungry.

'Have you done better than Special Branch, Doyle?' asked Cowley from his position of moderate comfort in Doyle's cord-covered, aluminium-framed easy chair.

'I don't think SB can have been properly watching the man,' said Doyle. 'They certainly never spoke to the copper outside.'

'Co-operative?'

'Very.' Doyle gulped coffee, smacked his lips appreciatively, then flopped into a second chair. 'Cards. Definitely cards. Our Rahad loves his flutter on the turn of the blind. Goes regularly to a variety of clubs for his game, but mostly, as you thought, to the Mayfair.'

'Nice to have it confirmed,' said Cowley gruffly. 'But he must have a . . .'

Doyle grinned boyishly. 'An Achilles heel, a little weakness? Right. Well he does and he doesn't. But if he does then it's blondes. Tall, leggy blondes. On the available evidence, extremely buxom blondes, who conform to a sort of total western stereotype.'

Cowley sipped his scotch, thoughtful. 'So his forte's as obvious as that, is it?'

'If forte's the word,' said Doyle. 'He has two or three a week, often the same girl coming back. Must be all that rice and sheep's eyeballs.'

Cowley chuckled, 'If it was, Doyle, then you and Bodie would eat nothing else yourselves.'

'Who, me, sir? What makes you think I need anything other than my natural, boyish charm?'

Cowley shook his head, still smiling. 'The girl told you most of this?'

'She couldn't wait to tell all. Apparently Rahad just sits around in the penthouse suite, waiting for orders, or instructions – never seems to work, she said – and when the girls come it's for most of the afternoon. The Embassy pays them handsomely, and he "tips" them. But they earn their money, from what she says.'

Cowley was thoughtful, his craggy features creased even more as he tried to sort out various implications. 'She came clean very easily.'

Smirking: 'Told her Rahad had a social disease.'

'Good God. And has he?'

'Yes sir. Cee-eye-five-itis.'

Cowley laughed loudly. 'I see. And is there any risk of feedback. From the girl to Rahad, I mean.'

'I think she got the message all right.'

'Blondes . . .' echoed Cowley, peering around the room as he said the word. He suddenly glanced sharply at Doyle. 'You said: he does and he doesn't have a weakness. What did you mean exactly?'

Doyle shrugged, unsure *exactly* what he meant, just acting on intuition. 'The girl thought that Rahad was easy about his women. He could take them or leave them. He took them whenever available, but didn't search them out, didn't get obsessed by them. He has a *taste* for blondes all right, but I'm not sure he's susceptible, slightly defenceless because of it.'

'I see.' Cowley drained his glass, rose from the chair. 'Then we'll have to be extra subtle. Thanks for the drink, Doyle.'

As he walked to the door, Cowley looked back over his shoulder at the moderate chaos behind him. 'Happy with your quarters?'

Surprised, Doyle shrugged. 'Sure.'

'Not too – luxurious for you?'

'Luxurious?' Doyle was incredulous.

'Aye, I know you like the spartan life.'

Cowley left, and Doyle closed the door behind him. He looked at his accommodation, hands on hips, head shaking gently. 'Luxurious, yet . . .' he repeated with a grin, then headed for the shower.

*　　*　　*

If there was an air of desperation on Bodie's smoothly handsome features, it was not solely due to the fact that he was *acting* the despondent loser. If his lips were tightly turned in irritation, if his dark eyes burned angrily, it was as much due to the fact that he *hated* to lose against such fat, ignorant men as he had played tonight.

He stood outside the back room of the casino, listening to the laughter, and the jocular comments at his own expense, of the two men who had cleaned him out. One was short and fat, a Welshman with a broad, sneering accent, who called Bodie 'boyo' and nearly learned the hard way not to call him that again. The other was smartly dressed, a man from the Middle East, low ranking, but wealthy. A man with connections, and Nero cultivated men with connections.

'Any time you want a return match, boyo . . . any time at all,' laughed the Welshman, and Bodie scowled and turned away. Again, tonight, the cards had run lucky for him, and how exasperating to have to throw them down, denying himself the chance to take a really big pot.

He had lost a grand, a thousand pounds, a whole thousand quid, and that made . . . over the days . . . nearly four thousand pounds in all. Who the hell was *financing* this phase of the operation? It appalled Bodie to think of such vast funds just waiting to be squandered on the likes of Nero and his fat-rat friends.

But Cowley had said to him that this operation was one of the biggest that CI5 had ever had to deal with. Not big in the sense of spectacular, just of immense importance to the Government. And a big operation in the sense that it was complex, like a game, a game in which every move depended to a great extent on a certain amount of luck.

Bodie himself was beginning to think that his luck was not in; perhaps his deliberately cultivated *bad* luck, his deliberate losing at cards, was affecting him body and soul. He was supposed to force an 'invitation' from Nero, an invitation to a much bigger game, but so far Nero had said not a word. Each game that was set up was in the same, sleazy backroom of the same sleazy club.

Bodie was getting frustrated. He found acting the same

role so many times a very tiring business.

Nero slapped him playfully on the shoulder, smiling broadly. 'I told you, man. I told you you'd be better off at home. But you just don't listen.'

'I like cards, Nero. I like to gamble. My luck must change, and when it does . . .'

Laughing uproariously, Nero walked round behind the bar. 'Man, you're *always* saying that. It's about time you started to face the fact that you was born *without* any luck.'

Bodie played along, shrugging, trying to look cheerful over his mournful features. He was hot and sticky in his evening jacket, and he undid an extra button on his shirt, wafted some cooler air down his warm skin.

'I want in on another game. Soon. Can you fix it?'

Nero shook his head, not as a gesture of the negative, but as a gesture of his endless admiration for the punter who didn't know when to quit. 'I can get a game, sure. Soon as you've got another stake . . .'

Bodie looked angry. 'I can get it! Last night, remember? Said I'd be back, didn't I? And I was, wasn't I?'

Nero stared at Bodie, hard, searching. The humour had gone from his face, now; suspicions were aroused and needed to be appeased.

'You're back all right,' said the black quietly. 'What do you do for a living, man? Steal purses from old ladies?'

'I get by,' said Bodie, wiping a hand across his mouth, looking tired, irritable. 'How about it, Nero, can you fix me up?'

'You dropped a packet, man. You've lost more in three days than I usually see lost in three weeks. You telling me your well never runs dry? Where d'you get the money?'

But Bodie just smiled, shaking his head: mind yours!

Nero finally shrugged. 'Well, let me think.' Looking at Bodie, weighing up the pros and cons of what he was about to do. He finally seemed to come to a decision, and nodded, just once, with finality. 'Okay, man. There's a game in town. A big game. Regular. But to get in, like, you've got to be near an astronaut.'

Bodie got the drift. 'No limit poker?'

'That's the name of the game. No limit, except they don't

flay the skin off you. What you got you spend. It's a big game, man. Well attended, heartbreaking.'

'That's the one I want in on.'

Nero seemed slightly concerned. As if he regretted having mentioned the game in the first place, now he back-pedalled. 'Hold on . . . I just *heard* of that game. I ain't saying I can get you in.'

Bodie sneered, 'Out of your class?'

Nero ignored the rudeness, glanced to where one of the dancing girls was walking across to him. She came up, looking tired, sweaty, dishevelled. In her skimpy costume Bodie could see that she was overweight and unfit, but Nero patted her on the backside and made an almost imperceptible sign with his eyes, upwards. The girl smiled thinly, staring at Bodie, then left the bar area. Her cheap perfume reeked, and Bodie's nostrils wrinkled in distaste.

Nero leaned on the counter. 'Not out of my class. I got connections.'

'Then start connecting.'

'Listen,' said Nero, just a touch of exasperation in his deep voice. 'You don't even get a chair in that game unless you got two grand stashed away . . .'

Shrugging non-committally, Bodie merely said, 'I can get that. No sweat.'

'Yeah? You tell me how, maybe we can do business.'

'I said I'll get it.'

Shaking his head, still very unsure of Bodie, Nero straightened up. 'Must have heard that a hundred times. "I'll get it. No sweat." Trouble is, most people don't get it all. That can be embarrassing. No, I'm sorry, mister. But if you want me to employ my connections, then you got to tell me how you'll raise the stake.'

Bodie appeared to give in, breathing slowly out, not looking at Nero for a moment as he weighed things up in his own mind. 'Okay. Have you heard of Sir John Terringham?'

'Sure have. He sweet on you?' Nero grinned as he said it, and Bodie responded with a faint grin of his own.

'Not him. His debby daughter Clare. I guess you know all about her too.'

Nero was impressed. 'Very top drawer. Very good people.

30

Very rich people. And exactly what *is* she ... to you, I mean?'

'Begging me to marry her ...' Bodie leaned back from the bar, more confident now. He let Nero digest the information, presenting the black with a self-gratifying little smirk, as if he was truly proud of the aristocratic fish he had hooked.

'Clare Terringham,' said Nero. 'Very tasty. She the one with the Roller? Dropped you here the other night?'

'You were looking,' said Bodie. 'You don't miss a trick.'

'Can't afford to, man.'

'Okay. So *I've* got connections. The question is, have you?'

Nero tapped the counter. 'Where can I reach you?' When Bodie looked uncomfortable about that, he went on, 'Look, this ain't something you set up just like that. I'll ask around ... and then get in touch. So give me a number where I can reach you. Trust me, man. I only want the best for you.'

He grinned, and Bodie, hesitating just briefly, finally scribbled a number on the flap of a cigarette packet.

'Don't keep me waiting, Nero. My luck has just *got* to turn good.'

Chapter Three

In any game, played seriously, there comes a moment when, in order to advance, a certain amount of discomforting back-pedalling must be applied. In chess, the sacrificing of a piece in order to claim a more valuable prize from the opposing side; in cards, perhaps, the underplaying of a good hand in order to keep the other players from knowing your true betting form.

In the game called 'Fix Rahad' the moment of discomfort came in the form of a touch of physicality, the acting out of aggression between Bodie and Doyle.

They couldn't fake it. They were professionals.

So one of them had to get hurt.

And early in the evening, on the day of Bodie's fourth disastrous card game, he and Doyle debated logically which of them was – literally – to be the fall guy.

The debate went like this: Doyle placed a coin on his thumb, then flicked his thumb and the coin span up to the ceiling.

Bodie called, 'Heads and I punch *you.*'

The coin clattered onto the floor, rolled a little and ended up beneath the armchair. They were in Bodie's apartment and Bodie shoved the chair backwards, bending to peer at the two-pence piece.

'Oh what a shame,' he said, with a broad grin on his face. 'On the other hand, it's about time my luck changed.'

'That was just a practice spin,' said Doyle, rather grimly. He picked up the coin. 'Best of three?'

Bodie just grinned and shook his head. 'I'm going to get rid of a lot of frustration in that single punch. Remember that time out at Marston Dale, where you caught me below the belt with your foot?'

'That was an accident,' said Doyle, shaking his curly hair, looking fervently at Bodie. 'Honest to God.'

'Then why did you laugh so much?'

'I always laugh when your voice rises an octave. Anyway, I was so distracted by having kicked you instead of the punter that the bugger clobbered me from behind.'

Bodie looked crestfallen. 'Damn, and I missed it.' He smirked, and then practised a side-sweeping punch. Doyle watched him and winced.

Touching the right side of his face, he worked his jaw about, then fingered around the area of his lower wisdom tooth. 'The thing is, I've got this loose filling. Soon as this job's over I'm going to get it fixed, but . . .'

Bodie raised a hand in a gesture of appeasement. 'Don't worry, Raymond. I shall hit you on the left.' He beamed, kissed his left fist and flexed the fingers. 'You won't feel a thing.'

'That's what I'm worried about,' said Doyle mournfully. Still holding his jaw he paced round the room. 'I mean, suppose they don't bite? It just doesn't seem fair. I'll be walking around chewing on one side and it'll all have been for nothing.'

'Not for *nothing*,' said Bodie, walking towards his small bathroom unit and stripping off his shirt. He looked back at Doyle. 'There'll be the pleasure factor for me. And you? Well, you'll just have to put it down to experience.'

'Thanks a bunch.'

Men who fight their way to the top, who struggle to achieve power, never exude that same aura of strength that is associated with the naturally powerful. The very rich, and the very intelligent, have an arrogance and a confidence that communicates invisibly, and marks them out as men to be reckoned with. But for the man of self-made power those trappings and signs of strength have to be gathered to his person, surrounding him, enfolding him in the manner of a security blanket.

Thus it was with Johnny Hollis.

To see Hollis on the street would not be to remark him; he was unremarkable, ordinary. He was a man of medium height, and although he had once been pugnacious and strong, he was now overweight and fleshy. His street life had been violent, grim, successful, and he had followed the natural progression up the ladder of power, from bodyguard, to trusted right hand man, to The Man of his own manor, controlling an area of London of quite staggering proportion; employing an army of heavies, and not so heavies, to keep his patch in order.

At the age of 40 he was desperately trying to retain his youth; he wore a toupee, cut in the style of the Beatles, a flop of hair around his skull, making him look more like a monk than a youngster. His face was red, his eyes puffy and deep set, ringed with the lines and shadows of excess. He wore an ostentatiously bright dressing gown, and open toed sandals, and he sprawled in a plush settee, hand on the upper, inner surface of a very young girl's mini-skirted thigh.

Around him were those trappings of power: the vast, expensively furnished suite, pictures, statues, antiques, chandeliers, all of them, in their way, exquisite; but combined to the tasteless requirements of a cultural and aesthetic *gaucherand* they appeared cheap, ineffective and just plain garish.

And of course, dotted among this cultural ineptitude were the brawny, sour-faced, humourless assistants, men of low background, negligible breeding, but of such physical strength that they could secure the inviolability of the Hollis corpus ... at least from any ordinary street fighter or northern Jimmy. Whether or not they could protect Hollis from the very cream of Organised Crime was a question that could be answered in only one way.

But for the moment, Johnny Hollis was comfortable, powerful, and very much in business. He had an empire that spanned from hard-core pornography to betting on the Test Match, and everything was going well; everything was paying.

The only thing he was short of was 'benders', his pet name for those men with a predilection for gambling who, at the same time, had an unfortunate predisposition to falling into debt. Such men were invaluable ... provided they held positions of power of their own. Inside men, inside information, influential contacts. . . . Hollis knew them all by the simple name of 'bender'.

34

And there was a chance coming up now, he understood, a chance to recruit a very interesting young man, someone with influence in the Land of the Aristocrat, that Land where *everything* was worth something.

The door at the far end of the suite opened and the squat figure of his right hand man, Martin Hart, appeared. 'You want to see him now, Mister Hollis?'

'Bring him in,' said Hollis, and turned away from the room to kiss the girl beside him. She reached round his neck to stroke the skin of his back, and Hollis's hand squeezed her leg tightly, then rubbed the red mark he had made. The girl never took her eyes off him, not even when Nero walked into the room and stood, about ten yards away, looking uncomfortable.

Hart went to the side of the room, sat down, and stared coldly at the black.

'Mister Hollis . . .' Nero said with a slight stutter.

Hollis turned away from the girl, smiled and waved at Nero. 'Tell me about this punter. Hart's told me something about him, but let's hear it from you.'

Nero rubbed his hands together, trying to stop them sweating. 'He's a real sucker, Mister Hollis. He loves cards, can't break the habit. He's been cleaned out four times now, straight and legal . . . no sharping. But each time he comes back for more, and each time with money.'

Hollis looked interested. 'Four times. And each time with a fresh roll. High money?'

'Grand a go. More the first night. Less on the last.'

'That's impressive.'

Nero seemed pleased. 'That's right. Well, Mister Hollis sir, like I was telling Mister Hart here, I've been cultivating the man. And he may be just about ready. I told him about the big game . . . and he bit . . .'

Hart looked round at Hollis, a certain earnestness on his flushed face. 'This sounds good to me, Mister Hollis.'

Hollis waved him silent, still staring at Nero. The girl nibbled his ear and Hollis smiled slightly. 'Think this man . . . what's his name?'

'Bodie. Just Bodie. Although I tend to call him "sucker".'

Nero laughed at his own joke, then grew solemn again as

35

no one else in the room laughed.

Hollis went on, 'Think this Bodie can raise the ante?'

'I'm not sure sir . . . he's a bit of a mystery. But he moves in the right circles. Right now he's going out with Clare Terringham . . . very fancy, very debutante. Rich people.'

'Clare Terringham,' repeated Hollis, and his eyes narrowed as he set his head back a little, staring at the ceiling. 'Nice choice of woman. Nice connection. The father's a big wheel in the Foreign Office. And the whole family is stinking, stinking rich.'

Enthusiastically, Hart rose to his feet and crossed the room to stand by Nero. 'His place must be worth ripping off, and if this Bodie . . . if he can be our inside man . . . ?'

Hollis stared at the two of them. Hart was eager to hit the Terringham country residence, and Nero clearly was eager to have pleased. Hollis felt disappointed in his business associate Hart. 'We'll check him out,' he said coolly. Hart looked nonplussed. But then Hart didn't understand the finer nuances of the business in which he found himself.

Hart said, 'Check him out? What's to check? Come on, Mister Hollis, you heard Nero. This Bodie's running around with the daughter. He visits their house in London. He *must* visit their country place as well . . .'

Interrupting him angrily, Hollis said, 'How many stretches have you done, Hart? How many times they put you away?'

Hart went pale, looked uncomfortable. 'Five. Five times.'

'And how many stretches have *I* done?'

'None, Mister Hollis. None at all.'

'Because I'm careful. Because I never rush in.' He grinned and turned towards the young girl. 'Do I? I never rush in.' Back to Hart. 'I check things out. I think things through. And that's what you're going to do now. You're going to get out on the street and check out this Bodie geezer. And think about what you're doing, and check him out good.'

Glumly, feeling patronised and put in his place, Hart nodded and said, 'Yes sir.'

Hollis added, 'And give Nero something. You've done well, Nero. You've done the right thing. I'm very pleased. From now on this Bodie is our stiff.'

36

'Thank you, sir. Thank you Mister Hollis.'

Hollis caressed the girl, who responded with a pouting embrace to his cheek. 'Right things have to be rewarded, eh?'

Slumped down in the seat of the Triumph Dolomite that he'd signed out of the pool, Ray Doyle watched the outside of Bodie's apartment block, not failing to notice the increasing anguish on Bodie's face each time he appeared at the top of the steps, making his way down to his Capri.

In three trips in and out of the block, Bodie had carried down all of his Hi-Fi equipment, and placed it on various seats in his car. Ready to sell it.

Doyle really felt for his partner at this point. He knew how much Bodie valued his Hi-Fi equipment, how many years he had spent building it up, what lengths he had gone to to build a sound system comprised of the absolute best, from amplifier to speakers, down to the tiny video-screen linked into the amplifier. The equipment was Bodie's pride and joy, second only to his sporting trophies.

It must have been breaking his heart to sell it; he must have been hating Cowley very much at that moment.

Eventually the car was loaded, and Doyle drove out to follow the Capri as Bodie violently swung into the road, and began the short drive to the only pawn shop he could depend on not to sell his stuff immediately.

Watching in his rear-view mirror, Doyle was delighted to notice a white Cortina pull into the road behind him, the man behind the wheel wearing sunglasses and looking *very* obvious.

He reached down for his radio and as unobtrusively as possible raised it to his mouth. 'Come in 3.7. Stop snivelling.'

Ahead of him he saw Bodie glance into the mirror, then make the almost unnoticeable shoulder movement that told of his R/T being raised to lips.

'If this equipment gets so much as scratched . . .'

'Good news, 3.7. I won't have to put your gentle tap down to experience.'

Bodie's voice was low. 'Someone bite?'

'Indeed they did.' Doyle again loked in his mirror. The
Cortina was keeping its distance, but had twice overtaken
another car to keep just Doyle's Dolomite between it and the
Capri that Bodie was driving.

'He's pretty good, using me for cover. White Cortina. Can
you see him?'

'I see him. You look a bit obvious with the radio.'

Doyle lowered his arm slightly. Speaking a bit louder he
said, 'Time for me to split. I'll see you at Terringham's
house . . .'

He placed the radio on the seat beside him and began to
indicate left, turning off the main road at the first oppor-
tunity, watching in his mirror as Hart's Cortina continued
on in pursuit of Bodie.

As he maintained the simple surveillance of the man called
Bodie, Martin Hart became more and more irritable. He
was still sore at having been so abruptly put down by Hollis.
Damn the man, who did he think he was? He and Hart were
from the same streets, the same class. What made Hollis so
jumped up? So the man was careful, and Hart had learned,
by bitter experience, the need for discretion. So what? When
Hollis finally got shopped he'd die . . . he'd die in the cells,
unused to the stench of confinement, the roughness of
prison blankets, the chewy, tasteless crap that was served as
food.

Hart wasn't at all sure that Hollis was the better man.

But Hollis *did* control the shots. At the moment. For the
time being.

It was clear enough to Martin Hart what this rough-
looking punter Bodie was up to. Hocking his music gear –
good quality stuff by the looks of it, probably worth half the
ante into the big game – and Hart would have been
prepared to swear that Bodie's next stop would be the
Terringham house for the soft touch on Clare Terringham,
and he wasn't thinking anatomically.

You didn't need brains to figure out the moves of a card-
addict like Bodie. Still, it was good to know the man was
serious about the game. And straight.

And obviously right for the gentle persuasion to play

against an IOU. And lose.

True to form, Bodie pulled up-outside a large Hi-Fi shop in Tottenham Court Road. Ignoring the double yellow lines, he transferred his gear into the shop, and about ten minutes later emerged counting a thick handful of money. He'd acquired a parking ticket, which Hart had avoided by driving quickly around the block.

The sale over, Bodie then drove round the block himself, and began to head westwards, towards the classy part of town where the Terringhams had their London residence.

The house was in a square, overlooking a small, meticulously maintained park. On four storeys, painted cream, with balconies on all the upper levels, Hart's mouth watered even more as he thought of the riches represented by that extravagant property. Bodie could well turn out to be a real find.

Again ignoring the fact that parking was not permitted in this narrow street, Bodie stopped his Capri and bounded up the steps to ring the front doorbell of the residence.

Hart drove a few yards on and, screened by a tree, stopped. He opened his window and leaned out, watching Bodie carefully, listening. He could hear every word that was said. The day was bright and still and sound carried on the breeze.

Bodie asked for Clare Terringham and was told that she wasn't in. Could he have a word with Alison Terringham? Mrs Terringham was not available for the moment. Perhaps Mister Bodie would like to return later in the day?

It sounded distinctly (to Hart) as if Bodie were being given the bum's rush from a household that was less keen on him, perhaps, than was the daughter of the house.

Looking distinctly grim, Bodie trotted down the steps, stood at the bottom for a moment, hands on hips, looking around as if trying to decide where to go next . . .

That was when the car appeared, screeching to a halt outside the Terringham house, stopped in the middle of the road.

There was something familiar about that car, but Hart never made the connection. He was too absorbed with the little scene that followed.

If I don't get an Oscar for this, thought Ray Doyle as he leapt from the Dolomite, I'm going to give up show-biz.

Then he went into his well-rehearsed routine, running up to Bodie and grabbing him by the shoulders.

He felt anger, irritation . . . he almost felt hate.

'You *stupid* idiot!'

'Shove off, Ray, for Christ's sake.' Bodie, startled to see his colleague, shrugged Doyle's hands from his shoulders, tried to walk back to his Capri.

Doyle swung him round violently, almost shouted at him.

'She's not your kind of woman . . . look at yourself, Bodie! She's out of your class! You're making a fool of yourself . . .'

Bodie pushed Doyle away, shouted back, 'Mind your own *business,* Ray! Butt out. You get on my nerves sometimes. Always trying to tell me what's good for me!'

Again Doyle yanked him to a stop, intensely earnest, desperately trying to talk some sense into his mate. 'She's the daughter of a rich man. They *play* with suckers like you, they like their bit of rough, then they tire of the game. It's a mug's game, Bodie. Can't you see that? She doesn't want you, she wants the excitement that you represent . . .'

'Now we're a psychologist, are we? Piss off, Ray. I've got enough problems at the moment without your heavy-handed, Mummy's boy advice.'

As Bodie walked away from him, Doyle taunted, 'Your gambling's going to finish you. You know that, don't you? You ain't the same man I started working with . . . you're just a cheap shot, no account, useless card-addict.'

Bodie turned and came back to face his partner. 'If you tell anybody, Ray, I'll bloody break your neck.'

Disgusted Doyle turned away, 'Tell anybody? You think they don't know? Christ, Bodie, there are none so blind as those who can't see what asses they're making of themselves. *I* know, and others know as sure as hell's hot. You're *dumb,* Bodie. You're gambling your life away . . .'

'Nobody knows, Ray, nobody except for you. And you won't tell, will you?'

'Give it up,' Doyle yelled. 'We used to be mates. But this

bug that's got you, and this fetish for rich broads . . . *not on,* Bodie. *Not cool.'*

'You tell anybody . . .' Bodie repeated menacingly, and in a fit of irritation Doyle swung his fist. Bodie blocked the blow and lammed Doyle with a left hook that sent the man sprawling.

Bodie turned on his heel and climbed into his Capri, roaring off round the square, not even looking at the hunched figure of Martin Hart as he passed.

Hart almost started to drive in pursuit, but a thought occurred to him and he swivelled round again to watch as the curly haired man climbed to his feet, cradling his jaw, dusting himself off, and eventually got back into his car.

As the Dolomite passed, Hart eased out onto the road again and followed the new arrival. Ahead of him, cradling his bruised jaw, Ray Doyle couldn't help himself . . . he gave a smug little smile of satisfaction as he noticed the white Cortina in indiscreet pursuit.

Back at his own apartment, Ray Doyle placed his jacket carefully over the back of an armchair, then went into the kitchen and filled a kettle with water.

He checked out of the window and saw the white Cortina parked close by. The driver was already on his way across the road.

Grinning, then wincing as pain shot through his bruised left jaw, Doyle rammed the whistle on the kettle and set it on the stove to boil.

'How do you do it, George?' he said aloud, impressed by the way George Cowley had figured that it would be Doyle that was pursued after the observed fracas, and not Bodie.

Every detail worked out; every contingency worked through.

'The man's a miracle worker.'

The doorbell rang and Doyle hesitated, checking the flat quickly, trying not to overlook the smallest detail. His jacket . . . ID in the jacket . . . kettle scheduled to boil in three or four minutes.

Perfect.

With a spring in his step he crossed to the door, then

assumed a slightly hang-dog expression – hand on jaw – as he pulled the door open.

The fat man who stood there bustled into the apartment, pushing Ray Doyle aside rudely, then turning on him.

'All right. Where is he?'

Doyle frowned, looking both startled and irritated. He slowly closed the door, then squared up to the intruder.

'Where's who?'

'That friend of yours: Bodie . . . I was told . . .'

Instantly Doyle reacted with violence, reaching out and grabbing the man's lapel, half lifting him from the ground. Although the fat man gave slightly, Doyle could sense the strength in his opponent, and knew that part of the sudden capitulation of his guest was due to the same sort of play-acting that he and Bodie had just indulged in.

The man said, 'No need to get rough,' and when Doyle released him he smoothed down his jacket, and cast Doyle a sly glance. Doyle noticed, though pretended to be depressed and rather distracted.

'What d'you want with Bodie?'

'Just what he owes me,' said the man. 'Nothing more. Nothing heavy. Just what the man owes me. Fifty quid. And he promised me . . .'

Doyle was exasperated, 'You too! Christ, how many more? Why the hell come here, though? I'm not the bloody man's keeper?'

The man shrugged. 'Heard you were a friend of his . . .'

Defensively, Doyle said, 'Friend? I wouldn't say that. We just work together that's all. Mates of a sort, but not close friends.'

The man clearly didn't believe him, having witnessed the emotional scene earlier. 'Work together, do you? Well you certainly don't mine for gold, that's for sure. He's not here then?'

Doyle shook his head. 'Has his own place. Fifty quid you said? How'd you get into him for that, as if I need to ask . . .'

'Dropped it in a card game last night. He was supposed to have paid up first thing this morning.'

'The damned fool!'

Doyle walked into the room and the stranger followed,

glancing around, taking it all in, trying to discern just what it was that Doyle and Bodie were into by way of profession.

He said, 'He promised to pay me. See it my way, I'm not made of money. He let me down.'

Doyle made a sound, as if he were astonished. Eyes wide he stared at his guest. 'Let *you* down. Ker-*rist!* He's let down more people than you can imagine.'

Almost exactly on cue the kettle started to whistle. Doyle said, 'Hold on.' He walked away from the man, into his kitchen, and vanished from sight. He called back, 'Fancy a cuppa, Mister, er . . .'

'Hart. And, er . . . no thanks.'

Hart walked across to the jacket where it lay over the back of the armchair. Continually glancing towards the kitchen, he picked the garment up, and checked swiftly through the pockets. He found Doyle's ID and flipped it open.

As he saw that Doyle was a CI5 man his eyes popped, his face blanched. He had heard of CI5. Tough boys; no nonsense types. Quickly, Hart placed the wallet back in the jacket, and returned the jacket to its position just as Doyle stepped back into the room holding a steaming mug. There was just the hint of a smile on Doyle's face, but it may – Hart reasoned – have been an angry twitch.

Hart was confident that his little bit of exploration had gone unnoticed.

'Work together then, do you? You and Bodie?'

Doyle swigged tea. 'Yeah. Have done for years. Sure you won't have a cup of tea?'

'Quite sure, thanks. Er, you and Bodie. What is it, then, same line of business? I mean, you do the same job do you?'

'Exactly. Partners you might say. If you're fishing for what exactly it is we do, you can stop fishing. 'Cos I ain't telling.'

Hart backed off, smiling thinly. 'Sure. It's just that I want some reassurance that he can pay.'

Doyle shrugged. 'Yeah, I can understand that. Look, he's going through a bad patch. Give him a few more days . . . I'll lean on him . . . maybe you'll get your money.'

The man called Hart nodded appreciatively. 'That sounds good. Okay, I agree. You've persuaded me. A few more days. Tell him he's got a few more days.' He turned to the door and Doyle could sense the smile on the man's face. But Hart was solemn as he glanced back: 'See you,' and then took his leave.

Doyle immediately drew out a folder of photographs and papers from the bottom drawer of his small desk. Spreading the photographs out he studied them again, noting the names, faces. He drew out the unflattering picture of Martin Hart and turned it over to read through the record and facts that were typed on the back. But before he replaced the picture in the folder he studied each photograph again: those of Rahad, looking arrogant, youthful; that of Johnny Hollis, the bewigged fat boy; Lucho, the helper; Nero, the black who ran the *Casino d'Or*.

They were all here in the file marked 'Fix Rahad'. Doyle again was amazed at the complexity of the operation, at the way disparate groups had been drawn together, weaved into Cowley's tangled web, with Cowley, the Black Widow, set right in the middle, a finger on every strand of the trap.

And Doyle and Bodie were the scampering insects at the edges of the net, setting up situations – like a political activist called Taylor who now 'owed' Doyle a favour – getting ready to initiate the next phase of an operation that would rapidly pass from being merely 'risky' to being downright dangerous.

In fact, at that precise moment Martin Hart was speeding back through London, to the penthouse suite where Johnny Hollis was waiting for him, his blood bubbling with excitement. Bodie was a real coup, provided they could count that coup upon him. What he had learned at Doyle's place put a whole new complexion on the matter . . .

He fairly ran down the corridor to Hollis's apartment. Pushing past the heavies by the door, he arrived breathless and sweaty, and waited impatiently for word to reach Hollis in the softly lit bedroom.

Hollis emerged, wearing his robe, the pantie-clad girl walking on his arm looking sullen and irritable; interrupted at her work, no doubt.

It didn't matter. This was far more important.

'Well. . . ?' prompted Hollis, pouring a large brandy into

44

a glass. Hart thought it might have been for him, but he was mistaken. Hollis sipped the drink himself and returned to the endless caressing of the girl on the settee.

'I reckon you can forget the Terringham house . . .' Hart blurted out, and Hollis frowned.

'That's a shame. What happened?'

'This Bodie character couldn't get past the butler this morning. It's the old story if you ask me . . . young feller reaching too high, playing outside his own league. Running with the rich girl he can't keep up with.'

Irritably, Hollis said, 'I get the general idea. So what happened?'

'I reckon she's pushed him over, given instructions not to let him in. He looked really fed up, very anxious. He raised a good bit of cash on some equipment he pawned, but I reckon he's stuck for the rest of the ante for the big game.'

'Then why in God's name,' said Hollis loudly, almost threateningly, 'Are we even bothering to talk about the creep? He's no use to us if he can't get us into the Terringham house . . .'

Hart played his master card, stepping forward, shaking slightly. 'Oh but he is, Mister Hollis. He is. And I'll tell you for why. He's in over his head, right? Hocking his stuff to stay there . . . but he's only got one way to go, and that's down . . . his salary isn't up to it, you see . . .'

Hollis frowned. 'How d'you know that?'

'Well I don't for sure,' blurted Hart, 'But I don't suppose that a CI5 man gets paid as much as a debutante would like these days . . .'

Hollis had jumped to his feet, walked across to Hart and stood staring at him. 'CI5! Are you sure?'

Hart grinned. 'Sure as I'm standing here, Mister Hollis. With a bit of good playing, and some bad luck for Bodie, you'll have yourself an inside man, all right . . . inside CI5!'

Hollis turned away from his man and walked back to the girl on the couch. As he bent towards her, rubbing and stroking her legs, he was already laughing, a loud, delighted sound that made everyone else in the room start to laugh as well.

Chapter Four

Ray Doyle needed a girl, and he didn't know how to go about finding one.

That apparent ignorance would have been unforgiveable if the girl he was seeking had been a girl of the ordinary sort. But what Ray Doyle wanted was a young woman whose physical attributes conformed to a very specific set of requirements, and whose professional capabilities made those attributes useful to CI5.

The classy hooker circuit was unfamiliar territory to Ray Doyle, less so to Bodie, no doubt, but Bodie had his own tasks to fulfil at the moment. So Doyle was on the street looking for a familiar face, someone to lean on, someone to help him out.

He was looking for George Flamini, and he found him in Notting Hill.

Flamboyant Flamini could be spotted half a mile off. He always dressed in a brilliant white, double-breasted suit, and black and white shoes. At his neck his tie was knotted so large that it looked like a green pouch below his chin. He was dusky-skinned, devastatingly handsome (and knew it well) with the rich, black, tightly curled hair of the Latin. Smouldering eyes, and an easy flashing smile, made him instantly attractive, instantly boring.

He was lounging against the sparkling white limousine that he had bought with practically every penny that he possessed, and that he used for various of his professional cons, solicits and capers with a great deal of success. He was a highly profitable one-man show . . . one man, one *woman* show, that is. The girl who sat in the limousine was an essential – some might say *the* essential – part of any Flamini operation.

Today, outside a posh hotel, a renowned business- and oil-man's gin-dive, he was operating the kid-sister routine.

He knew his audience, intuited the tastes of his potential customers with professional, pin-point accuracy. Older men liked younger girls; business men thought that the more they paid, the less experience (i.e. more virginal nerves) they could buy.

If the girl acted her part, and the price was high enough, the same girl might be convincingly deflowered twenty times a week.

The only difficulty was setting up the punter to take the bait.

Today, Flamini had worked brilliantly (if he *did* say so himself). Within minutes the nervous, greying man who would step out of the door would be chauffered to Flamini's erotic, exotic apartments with a trembling, blushing young girl in the back seat, a girl who would be calmed, relaxed, seduced, and made *woman* by the greying business man, whose pockets would be lighter to the tune of two hundred pounds.

Everything was going wonderfully.

So when a voice said softly, behind him, 'Hello George,' he smiled, turned, ready to greet the acquaintance.

And found himself facing the beaming, cheeky features of Ray Doyle; a pleasant enough sight to most people, it was the sort of startling vision that could put Flamini off his *escalope milanese* for a week, and give him nightmares to boot.

Flamini immediately panicked, the smile on his face replaced by an expression of terrified concern. Glancing at the hotel, then at the car, then at Doyle, he looked, for a moment, as if he would explode.

'Long time no see, George,' said Doyle cheerfully. 'How've you been, eh? Business good? Good. Get in the car, George. Want to have a little chat . . . '

Flamini resisted. 'Oh no, Mister Doyle. Please. Not now. Don't bust me now. *Please*!'

Doyle took him firmly by the arm, pushed him slightly towards the limousine. 'Get in the car, George.'

Still whining, still convinced that he was about to be busted, George Flamini stooped and entered the sumptuous interior of the car. Doyle followed, grinning broadly as he saw the girl sitting there.

She was huddled in the corner, looking anxiously from Flamini to Doyle. She was startlingly attractive, and dressed in girlish clothes, all whites and pinks, with little ankle socks. As Doyle peered closer, though, he could see the glossy lipstick, smell the heavy make-up. A real tart, he thought to himself.

Flamini was saying urgently to this sweet young thing, 'Say nothing. Absolutely nothing!'

'Wasn't going to ask her anything,' said Doyle, settling comfortably next to the Italian, and looking around. '*Very* smart, George. You certainly know a tasty car . . .'

'I bought this in the better times,' mumbled Flamini. 'Everything is legal. Everything above board.'

'I'm *sure* it is, George,' soothed Doyle. 'It isn't the car I'm here to talk about . . .'

Hands clasped together, Flamini took on the look of a man praying hard, eyes narrowed, pleading. '*Please* Mister Doyle! It's been a long, hard year, the dollar went down, did you hear that the dollar went down? And it took the yen along with it . . . I'm waiting for a score. He's about to come out now. The best John in months, and I can't afford to lose him . . .'

Doyle snickered, looking at the girl and saying mischievously, 'And he's into unspoiled virgins, eh?'

The girl reacted to that, frowning and saying loudly, 'Now look you!' Her voice was *terrible* – harsh, brassy, common. Doyle's eyebrows lifted, and he could barely stop himself laughing. No doubt, when the 'John' got into the car, her voice would be softer, more giggly and lisping.

What some people would do for kicks, he thought in amazement.

'Keep quiet little girl,' he said aloud, and turned to George, who simultaneously had shouted, 'Shut up!' to the unfortunate lass.

Doyle said, 'Look, George . . .'

But Flamini interrupted him, again urgently, 'Mister Doyle, *please*! Tomorrow I'll come in and surrender – anything you say . . . but not today, don't bust me today . . .'

'I'm not going to bust you, George.'

Flamini's face went blank, his stare like the look of an amazed trout. 'You're not?'

Doyle slapped him in friendly fashion on the shoulder.

'Bust you, George? Why would I want to do a thing like that. All I want from you, George, is a . . . how shall I put this. I want a girl. *You* know . . .' he nudged the man painfully and Flamini sat bolt upright, still staring in astonishment.

'You want a girl. *You?*'

'Me,' echoed Doyle pleasantly. 'I'm only human, George. I want a girl, someone with class, real class . . .'

The painted virgin leaned forward more interestedly, now. 'Won't I do?' she said in broad East London tones. She smiled.

The smile vanished as George Flamini's hand slapped her gently across the mouth. 'He said class, now shut up!' Back to Doyle. 'Are you *sure* this isn't a bust?'

'Cross my heart.'

Flamini thought hard for a moment. 'All I run is tramps.' The girl behind him squealed with indignation. 'You want The Lady. She runs the classiest string of girls in town.'

Doyle leaned closer. 'Can you fix it for me?'

Flamini shrugged. 'Sure thing. I'll have her send someone over. Your place?'

Doyle scribbled the address on a scrap of paper. Flamini asked, 'When do you want her?'

'As soon as possible,' said Doyle. 'Tonight. And listen, tell The Lady that I want a natural blonde . . . long hair . . . tall . . . I definitely want long legs, plenty up top . . .'

'How about her teeth, you want good teeth?'

'Don't be facetious, George.'

Flamini shrugged and grinned. His eyes now, were fixed almost permanently on the exit from the hotel. There was still a chance to score, if only Doyle would go. 'Okay,' he said, 'I'll fix that for you. You want class, you'll get class. Now give me a break, Mister Doyle . . .'

Grinning, Doyle left the car. Flamini shuffled across the seat and breathed a great sigh of relief, wiping his face with a handkerchief.

Behind him the girl started to sniffle. 'What's the matter with you.'

'You called me a tramp.'

Irritated beyond all responsibility, Flamini shouted 'Shut

49

up!' Turning back to the hotel he saw the astonished, puzzled face of his 'John', frowning at him, then shaking his head and walking quickly away.

Flamini's cry of frustration echoed through Notting Hill.

Bodie and Cowley were sitting across a coffee table from each other, laying cards down in swift succession, concentrating hard on the moves, on the value of the faces that were shown; it was warm in Bodie's apartment, and a half bottle of scotch stood close by to the two men as they played, empty glasses testifying to the fate of the other half.

The game was at stalemate when suddenly Bodie yelled with glee, and cried 'snap', pulling the great pile of cards towards him.

The telephone rang.

He and Cowley exchanged a long, thoughtful stare. Cowley said, 'This'll be it.'

Bodie stood and crossed to the phone, plucked it from its cradle and, licking his lips, said, 'Yeah?'

Nero's deep voice greeted him, in the background the sound of music suggesting that the club was already in full swing so early in the long day.

'What have you got for me, Nero?'

Nero said, 'I spoke to the man. And you're in.'

Bodie gave a thumbs up to Cowley who nodded, satisfied, and sat back in his chair.

Down the phone, Bodie said, 'This is the big one, is it? I'm not interested in any penny-ante games.'

'This is the big one,' agreed Nero. '*If* you can raise the ante, which is two grand.'

Bodie said, 'I'll raise it. When's the game. And where?'

Nero chuckled. 'It ain't worth my hide to let you know that just yet. I'll call you again. It'll be soon.'

The line went dead. He stared at the receiver for a moment, then placed it gently back in its cradle. Looking up at Cowley he nodded his head. 'You said it would happen fast, and you were right.'

Cowley stood, hands in his pockets, and went to look at Bodie's collection of trophies. 'Standard procedure, Bodie.

You're a very fine mark, to them, and they want to get their hooks into your money before someone else does.'

He walked to where his coat lay, folded neatly across the back of an armchair.

Bodie looked a little sullen as he watched his boss. 'Am I allowed to *win* anything this time? Do you know what it's like losing so often.'

Cowley looked at the cards on the table, shook his head. 'Aye, I do. I feel humiliated . . . ' he grinned.

Bodie said. 'Their games aren't snap. I could have made a small fortune on the last few nights. Those boys are definitely second league.'

Cowley fixed him with that steady, crinkled Cowley stare, assessing his operative, noting the growing signs of frustration . . . and weakness.

'Be strong, Bodie. The game you'll go to will probably *let* you win for a few hands. That'll be even worse. When the high hand comes you'll know you've been set up. You'll lose. Lose badly. It's not your money they want . . . '

'Yeah, I know. It's me. I hope you've got my Hi-Fi back safely. With two broken legs it'll be the only pleasure I get.'

Cowley opened the door to the flat, smiling. 'It won't come to that, Bodie. These snakes are taking our bait, mouthful after mouthful. Keep your cool, act the part well. I'll be back before you leave for the game. With the ante. Right now, I have to see a man about a girl!'

As Bodie looked surprised, the door closed behind Cowley.

Bodie shook his head. 'He's enjoying this too much.'

The girl was due to arrive at eight in the evening.

An hour before that, Doyle fussed around his apartment, tidying it up, trying to get rid of the faint aroma of the fried duck with pineapple on which he and Cowley had gorged themselves earlier. He had no idea what to expect, but imagined someone better spoken, though equally made-up, as the girl who was working for George Flamini. He had therefore laid in a supply of soaps, creams, and delicate face towels, ready to inspect the girl in her natural form. It had been Cowley's idea, of course.

Cowley was playing the game with precision.

Ray Doyle actually had butterflies in his stomach as the appointed hour arrived. He couldn't think why. It made no sense at all. Perhaps it was because the girl who was about to arrive would be one of the most highly paid call-girls in London, and could afford to be choosy, was probably terrifyingly experienced, and in one sense way out of *his* class.

The doorbell rang and he crossed to open it. And if his eyes widened as he looked at the girl who stood there it was not because she looked the part of the highly-paid tart, but because she was so natural, and naturally beautiful.

She was certainly tall, dressed in a knee-length skirt and silk blouse, dressed tastefully, and expensively; her face had only the merest hint of make-up on it, a touch at her wide, shining eyes, a hint of colour on her high cheekbones. Her blonde hair was meticulously crimped, and exquisite to regard.

There was just a hint of shyness in her, a flutter of girlish nervousness as she said, 'Mister Doyle?'

Doyle wasn't taken in by that touch of professional acting, but he still managed to fall slightly under her spell. 'You're not . . . ? Are you . . . ? You don't look . . . '

The girl smiled genuinely. She looked slightly amused by Doyle. 'We don't stand under lamp-posts swinging our purses any more.' Looking around at the passageway she added. 'Do you want me to come in, or do you have something in mind out here in the hallway?'

Doyle stood to one side, 'Sorry. Come in. Please.'

The girl walked into the apartment, glanced around, then turned to face Doyle. When she moved she seemed to glide, hips not rolling in an exaggerated way, every part of her seeming poised and elegant.

'The Lady sent me. You can call me . . . well, whatever you like, really.'

Doyle smiled. 'How about Anna?'

'A *very* pretty name,' laughed the girl. 'So I'm Anna for the night. How nice.' She turned from Doyle, walked deeper into the room, obviously not impressed. Suddenly she sniffed. 'Chicken and pineapple?'

Doyle stared at her curiously, then shook his head. 'Duck!'

'None left, I suppose. I'm starving.'

'Sorry. Big appetite myself.'

He was still standing by the door, staring at the girl, unsure of how to react to her. He was turned on by her, by her looks, by the fact that she was incredibly sexy . . . and by her naturalness. If she was acting the part of a girlfriend, she was excellent at it.

Anna caught the stare, placed her bag on the coffee table and stared back. She turned from the right to the left, swivelling at the knee, looked coy, shook her hips, shook her bust, and said, 'You did specify someone *classy*. If I don't measure up then my finishing school has a lot to answer for.'

She was certainly well spoken, her voice possessing that rounded accent that Doyle always associated with the landed gentry of the Home Counties.

But finishing school? 'You're kidding,' Doyle said. 'You must be kidding.'

'Why should I be doing that?' The girl's cool and poise never wavered, but a note of slight irritation had crept into her voice. 'Listen, if you want me to act a part, that's fine. Tell me and I will. But unless you specify what you want, then what you'll get is the real me. Except for my name . . . '

'Sorry,' said Doyle, placatingly. But now Anna looked a little amused with him.

'You're shocked, aren't you? Or at least, surprised. But I can't think why. I was told you work in a very tough business.' She frowned, puzzled by the man. 'But you *are* shocked. It's very refreshing . . .' Her smile suddenly vanished. 'Or is it that you're disappointed?'

'Disappointed? What, in you?'

'Perhaps I'm not classy enough?' A bit of a pout, a touch of deliberate concern.

'No way,' said Doyle with a grin. 'No way am I disappointed. Well, one way, perhaps, but you'll find out what that is. Would you like a drink?'

'Oh, yes please. I'm gasping. A very bloody Mary if you don't mind.'

'Right.'

Doyle went to his drinks cupboard and found his half

53

bottle of vodka. He had one tomato juice left. He poured a scotch for himself, watching Anna from the corner of his eye as he did so. She prowled about the room just once, then sat down, folded her skirt very carefully across her knees, and stared at Doyle.

Doyle brought the drinks across. 'Cheers.'

She raised her glass, sipped the bloody Mary and made a sound as of satisfaction. 'Your good health,' she said. 'May your stamina peak.' She giggled.

Doyle sat opposite her, crossing his legs. 'Do you ride?' he asked.

Anna nodded vigorously as she sipped her drink. 'Mm, yes. I love riding. I ride very well, as a matter of fact . . .' she hesitated, then, and glanced quizzically at Doyle. 'You *do* mean horses?'

Doyle laughed. 'Yes. Horses. I did mean horses. I like riding as well. Don't get much chance, though.'

'I belong to two stables. Often go on pony treks on my father's estate in Cumberland. Exhilarating.'

Ray Doyle said nothing for a moment, regarding the girl carefully, liking what he saw immensely. Then he said, 'Parlez vous français?'

Anna's eyes widened, then she frowned, then she said, 'Oui m'sieur. Je parle français, et je le parle meilleur que vous. Votre accent est abominable.' As Doyle grinned, again she frowned, and in English said. 'Er, when you ask me if I speak French, you do mean . . . ?'

'Yes, I do mean the language. Is my accent really that bad?'

'Terrible. Like a Monty Python Frenchman.'

'Oh wonderful.' Doyle sipped his scotch, then smiled broadly and said, 'Well, that's pretty nigh perfect. You ride, you speak French . . . your father is landed gentry. You could almost be a debutante.'

Anna shrugged, as if to say, what do you mean 'almost'? 'As a matter of fact I was. I keep telling you, Mister Doyle, I have a background. I'm class. You keep thinking I'm acting the part.'

'A debutante hooker . . .' mused Doyle, and shook his head. 'Doesn't seem to fit.'

Anna shrugged. 'It's all a question of degree, Mister Doyle. When I was sixteen I used to sleep with older men in return for a champagne dinner, and a good disco session. When I was eighteen I'd sleep with anybody at all, provided they lived on a country estate and could get me a long weekend of salmon fishing, riding and eating off silver plates. At twenty I nearly slept with someone who was dangling 'Lady of the Manor' in front of me. Now that I'm twenty-one I just do it all for the money. And occasionally for the fun.' She raised her glass, the drink nearly gone. 'Cheers.'

After a moment, Anna looked over her shoulder at the closed door to the bedroom. 'Well, Mister Doyle. Do you want to sit here and talk for a while? Or would you rather we took our *second* drinks through to the bedroom and . . .' Her eyebrows rose, and her lips parted slightly in an inviting smile.

Doyle said, 'Ah. Okay, this is where we come to the funny part.'

Anna frowned. 'Oh. I see. Well I should tell you, before you go on, that anything *too* kinky is out . . .'

'It's nothing like that,' said Doyle. 'What I have to propose is a straightforward business arrangement. Good pay for a good piece of acting on your part . . . with professional activities thrown in, of course.'

Anna placed her glass down on the table, and leaned on her knees, her eyes wide as she stared at Doyle. 'Now I *am* kinky when it comes to money. What did you have in mind?'

'I want you to do a very special favour . . . for a friend of mine . . .'

As he said this, the bedroom door opened and the tall, smiling form of George Cowley stepped through. Anna gasped, obviously startled, then relaxed again and stood up. 'Two of you?'

Cowley shook his head. 'Neither of us, Miss . . . er, Anna. A friend of ours, an Embassy man called Rahad. Sit down again . . .' He looked at Doyle. 'Drinks all round, please. While I tell Anna exactly what's required of her.'

Chapter Five

There would come a time, Rahad knew, when he would have
to return to his own country. When he did so there was one
thing he was determined to do: keep horses.

The thought of his homeland did not fill Rahad with
ecstasy; he was not homesick, did not hunger for the dry
heat, the slow pace of life, the exotic standard of living. He
had come to England in his teens and felt a part of this
country. He liked the climate, its pace, its night life. He
especially liked its aristocracy, into whose circle (the peri-
phery of which, at least) he had managed to buy and charm
his way.

No, he was at home in England, but he recognised that
the possibility of a return to the Middle East was always a
tangible threat. So if he *did* have to go, he would take his
money, his experience, and his contacts, and he would breed
horses.

It was one of his few pleasures.

In times of stress he had various ways of calming himself.
Today, on the day before an evening's gambling in Mayfair,
he had decided to ride his magnificent brown mare – Sultan
– through Hyde Park. It was not his favoured riding ground,
but there was no time to go out into the country for a truly
relaxing canter. Hyde Park would do well enough.

Sultan was restless, irritable; not able to be given its full
rein the animal snorted, whickered and paced too heavily on
the soft ground. Rahad worked hard to control the beast,
but occasionally cantered it, enjoying the feel of the wind on
his face.

The park was not busy; in full leaf, in the depths of the
area, it was almost possible to think you were outside
London, in the heart of the country. But the distant sound of
traffic was always there, and the tall shapes of buildings
could always be glimpsed through the trees.

Rahad had decided to keep a low profile for a few weeks. He was disturbed by the attention that had been paid to him by Special Branch, and by his meeting with George Cowley of CI5. If a net *was* being cast, he would do well to be a frozen fish for a while. Whoever had told Achmed Rajavi that he was to be assassinated (and he knew he would probably never find out exactly who had informed) had probably let that same information slip to the authorities. It had not saved Achmed's life, but it had caused the suspicious sniffing of the British police.

For a while, Rahad was doing the cultural attaché work for which he was ostensibly paid. He didn't enjoy it.

There were other horses in the park, all of them trotting their owners on short, circular tours through the trees, through the stretch of the park known as Rotten Row. Rahad recognised several of the riders and acknowledged them pleasantly.

A rider approached whom he did not know. She was dressed smartly in dark brown suede jacket, and beige jodhpurs, and she was cantering her horse towards him, looking expert and comfortable in the saddle. Rahad watched her approach, admiring the girl's figure, her clear, aristocratic beauty. He made ready to acknowledge her with a charming smile, but as she rode past she looked away.

Rahad shrugged, and smiled to himself, but in that same moment the girl's horse reared, and she cried out.

Rahad reined his own horse round, and saw the girl fighting to stay in the saddle, desperately trying to soothe her mount, which was kicking and rearing, and seemed to have been panicked by something, possibly a dog.

As it finished panicking, so the horse began to bolt, the girl leaning forward over the nape of the neck, clinging on for dear life.

Rahad kicked Sultan in pursuit, galloping swiftly up to the scared horse and its pale faced, shocked rider. He reached across and took the halter firmly in his hand, then spoke loudly and commandingly to Sultan, and the horse slowed, shaking its head, but in perfect control. The girl's horse slowed too, and in moments they were stopped by the track, the girl petting and calming her mount, Rahad, dismounting

57

and checking the animal's fetlocks.

'I'm very grateful,' said the girl, stepping down from the saddle and breathing a little heavily.

Rahad straightened and then bowed just briefly. 'Glad to have been of service.'

'I don't know what made him bolt. I didn't see a dog, and there can't be any snakes in Hyde Park, can there?'

Rahad smiled reassuringly. She was incredibly beautiful, this girl; her eyes shone with fire, and with pleasure. Her lips were full and moist; Rahad could smell the sweetness of her breath. His stomach knotted with desire.

'The horse bolted because you looked away from me as you went past. And there was I giving you my most winning smile.'

Corny, he knew, but he had little to lose. The girl seemed coy, smiling to herself, as if secretly pleased at the mild pass.

'I didn't look away deliberately,' she said. 'I swear I didn't. Snoopy seemed to be tense, not riding well, and I suppose I felt the shake-up coming.'

Rahad was chuckling. 'You call this beautiful animal Snoopy?'

The girl laughed too. 'Why not? He's a very self-possessed horse . . .'

Rahad grew solemn, a little more intense, 'And may I know the name of this beautiful creature?' As he spoke he pointed delicately at the girl. She blushed, lowered her eyes just quickly, then began to stroke the neck of her horse. 'My name's Anna.'

'A lovely name. I am Tefali Rahad. I work at an Embassy. I find London a very exciting place . . . but it can be lonely. I dine at the most expensive restaurants, I know Ministers and Kings, I belong to the best clubs. But meeting you is the most exciting thing that has happened to me in months. Please forgive me for saying so, but you really are a delightful young woman.'

Smugly, he noticed that his romantic words had caused her to look at him, the look on her face being one of growing passion, melting resistance. She was pleased by his forwardness, but shy, too shy to respond brashly. Unless he said something else it might easily end right there, a chance encounter with an exquisite English girl.

He said, 'Have I embarrassed you?'

Anna said quickly, 'Oh no, not at all. I just . . . I just don't know what to say. I'm very flattered.'

Rahad smiled charmingly, extended his hand which Anna took and shook in that very proper, English way. Instead of letting go, however, Rahad kept the hand in his, gently squeezing the fingers. 'You could say that you would dine with me tonight. You could say that you would accompany me to the casino where . . . with you behind me . . . I am sure I can win a small fortune. And if I do . . . if I do, I shall buy Snoopy, here,' he patted her horse, 'a gold-plated horse box! Or should I say kennel?'

Anna laughed delightfully. Rahad laughed too.

'What do you say, lovely Anna?'

'I say . . . I'd love to. I'd love to dine with you.'

Rahad bowed low. 'Let's ride a little longer. Then I will escort you home.'

And as they rode away, deeper into the greenery of the park, Ray Doyle, watching through binoculars from his parked car couldn't help a wry smile touching his lips. 'What a smoothie,' he muttered to himself, lowering the glasses and sighing deeply. 'Damned if he isn't.'

Nero had kept Bodie waiting for twenty-four hours. Then he had rung to say that the game was fixed for that night, at eight o'clock. Had Bodie got the ante? Bodie had indeed. They arranged to meet outside the block of extravagant apartments in Mayfair where the game would be held: the suite would be that belonging to a London mobster called Johnny Hollis. Bodie, through George Cowley, already knew this.

He decked himself out in silk shirt, bow-tie and swish tuxedo. He felt good in the gear, quite fancying himself on the London casino circuit. He was a man of extremes, was Bodie; he was comfortable in jeans and leather jacket, recapitulating his athletic army days in long, exhausting pursuits on foot; he liked to dress up to the nines and haunt the more exclusive places of London, among a company of men who couldn't run twenty yards without puffing and blowing, even if it were the devil himself that pursued them.

Tonight, though, the occasion wasn't quite as classy as he would have liked. Exclusive, yes. But classy, definitely not.

So he reached to pick up his gun and holster, and was perturbed when George Cowley reached out before him and gently lifted the weapon away.

'I'd feel naked without it, sir.'

'You're hard enough without the hardware, Bodie. One look at you and eight per cent of Hollis's mob would run a mile.'

Bodie still felt uncomfortable. 'I thought you said they knew already I was with CI5.'

Cowley nodded, rugged face pale in the light of a corner lamp. 'All part of the game plan, Bodie. I know what you're thinking: they'll *expect* you to carry a gun. But the gun would be taken from you on your way in, anyway, so there's no point in arousing suspicions, or fears, more than we have to.'

Bodie glumly accepted that. He buttoned up his tuxedo.

'So tonight I lose and get recruited. Then what?'

'Then I play a move that is risky, unpredictable, and on which the whole success of this operation depends. Never mind about it now, Bodie. Just remember your instructions.'

Bodie nodded, then smiled. 'Going to wish me luck, sir?'

'Luck won't get us anywhere,' said the hard-faced Scot. 'Not luck . . . but maybe a little cunning.'

Cowley reached into his pocket and took out a thick wad of notes. He handed these to Bodie who smiled, slapped them into his hand, then pocketed them.

'Just the same sir . . . I wouldn't mind a bit of genuine lucky Scottish heather. I *am* the bait, after all.'

Cowley chuckled, turning from Bodie. 'My cousin put his back out reaching down for some lucky Scottish heather. I don't trust to luck. I trust to skill, to judgement. And I repeat . . . cunning.' He walked to the door, glanced back at his operative. 'Besides, you're not the bait, Bodie. You're the trap!'

Tefali Rahad could hardly believe his good fortune.

An hour before he was scheduled to leave for the poker

game in Mayfair, he found himself basking in the comfort of a penthouse suite made twenty times more cosy by the presence of his beautiful new acquaintance.

She had relaxed greatly during the early evening, wined and dined simply, but tastily, of the very best of the Embassy's cuisine. Every item of food had been an experience to her, and the relish with which she had eaten was almost erotic.

She had confessed to being slightly inexperienced in many ways. Rahad had promised to educate her in any ways she liked. Anna had responded to that with exactly the right words.

She was elegantly attired in a sleek, clinging evening gown, low cut, and semi-translucent, and when she stood against the light Rahad could feast his eyes upon the smooth, curved lines of her body. He almost regretted that the card game had been organised for this evening. But Anna had agreed to accompany him to Mayfair . . . and she would agree to return home with him afterwards.

Win or lose, tonight Rahad would be the winner.

'You know,' he said, pouring a little more ice cold champagne into her glass as she sat and looked at him. 'You know, Arabs believe in Fate. It is an integral part of our faith.'

Anna sipped champagne, watched Rahad coyly, sexily. 'You mean the way we met?'

Rahad sat down again, crossed his legs and feasted his eyes on the sublimely elegant figure of the girl next to him.

'I mean exactly that. You and I, meeting as we did . . . it was ordained. It was meant to happen. It was planned by a higher authority . . . '

He reached across to gently pat Anna's back as she choked delightfully on a mouthful of champagne. The touch of her bare skin sent a thrill through his whole arm. The girl recovered, touched her lips, flushed in the face, and smiled apologetically.

'Was it something I said?' asked Rahad with a laugh.

'Not at all. I was enjoying listening to you, and I wasn't concentrating on what I was doing. You were saying . . . about the higher authority . . . '

61

'Just that someone intended us to meet. This was no accident. It was part of a greater design.'

Anna nodded in all seriousness. 'I totally agree with you. I felt it myself.' She leaned across and gently kissed Rahad on the lips. Looking up at him afterwards, dark eyes moist and wide with desire, she whispered. 'I very much want you, Tefali. I hope the game is over quickly.'

Rahad shivered at the sound of her voice, at the magic of those seductive words. He raised Anna's hand to his lips.

'You will bring me luck tonight, I am sure of it. Yes, I have a feeling I will be very lucky tonight.'

The lift glided up towards the penthouse suite, and stopped so gently that Bodie hardly realised it had been in motion.

He looked at Nero, standing next to him, and gave a nervous little smile. 'You'll be okay, man,' said the black. 'You won't win, but you'll sure have a good time losing.'

Bodie smiled as Nero laughed. He had noticed a subtle change come over the Negro; the man seemed more friendly, almost as if he hoped Bodie would do well. He had even given Bodie a run-down on the heavies who would be hovering around the game, and on two of the other players. The run-down was unnecessary, as it happened, since Bodie had already been well-briefed by CI5. But it was comforting, in an odd sort of way, to know that Nero hadn't lied.

The game – Bodie felt – would be straight, on the whole. He didn't know why that gave him a little extra confidence, but it did.

The lift door opened and Nero ushered Bodie out into the palatial foyer of the penthouse suite. Thick carpeting, elegant lamp stands, pictures, drapes, flowers . . . the expensively appointed ante-chamber of a rich man.

'You had it right, Nero,' said Bodie. 'Way out of your class.'

Wryly, Nero said, 'More'n you think, man. Much more.'

There was a single apartment door leading off from the foyer, and Nero led the way across to it. He rang the buzzer three times, then three times more in quick succession.

Bodie recognised the burly, squat little man who opened the door to admit him. Martin Hart. He had seen the man hanging around the *Casino d'Or*. Behind Hart, moving towards him, was a gorilla of a man, about six six tall, broad as the Thames, and very dark jowled. Bodie flicked through his mental file of faces, and characters, and recognised with no difficulty at all the brainless, but extremely powerful Billy Lucho.

Lucho had never done time, even though he had been on CI5's files for years, and had been implicated in several criminal activities. Perhaps the reason was that Lucho resisted arrest more successfully than most.

Nero said, 'You're on your own now, Bodie. This is as far as I go.'

Bodie was slightly startled by that. 'Come on Nero. You're my luck.'

Nero shook his head. 'They don't allow no Blacks or Coloureds in the game.'

'There's a law against that,' said Bodie, glancing at Hart, who merely shrugged.

'Up here it's their law,' said Nero sourly, 'and I would say they had it stacked, wouldn't you?'

Bodie looked at the two burly men who stood before him and slowly nodded. 'He can't come in?'

Hart smiled and slowly agreed.

Nero said, slapping Bodie on the back, 'You do well, now. You show 'em!' And with that he turned on his heel and went back to the lift.

Bodie began to step forward, into the long, plush suite beyond the doorway, when Lucho placed a huge, hairy paw upon his shoulder and jerked him rudely, and uncomfortably, against the wall. Lucho held him there, quite motionless, as Hart swiftly and expertly frisked him. He found the money, looked at it, looked at Bodie and smiled, then popped the wad back into the pocket of Bodie's tuxedo.

'Come this way, sir,' said Hart sweetly, and Lucho turned to guard the door as Hart paced off across the apartment, Bodie dogging his heels.

The gambling room was a small area off the main lounge. Here was set up a table, covered by green baize, with chairs around it for four. Two lights shone down on the table, and the edge of the small room was shadowy. Bodie noticed two men already sitting there, but Hart took him first to the bar that was situated between lounge and gambling arena.

An attractive, very young girl wearing a low cut gown and too much make-up, smiled at Bodie from behind the bar. Bodie smiled back, gave her the once over and found her to his liking.

Johnny Hollis appeared from another room, decked out in similar tuxedo and shirt to Bodie. He looked smart, relaxed, but overweight and unfit. His toupee was not quite straight and caused the hint of a smile to touch Bodie's lips.

Hollis didn't appear to notice, extended his hand and greeted Bodie warmly. 'Mister Bodie, so glad to meet you.'

'You too,' said Bodie, glancing back at the girl behind the bar.

'I hope we're able to give you some sport tonight. Would you care for a drink?'

'Thanks. Scotch on the rocks.'

Hollis glanced at the girl. 'Tina ... scotch for Mister Bodie.'

As Tina turned away to find the bottle, Hollis steered Bodie into the small playing room. Bodie cast a last, furtive glance at Tina, before he was forced to give his attention to the two players already at the table.

'These are two of the gentlemen you'll be playing with tonight ... as long as your luck holds out. Er ... an American friend.' Hollis indicated a fat, balding man, who had stripped off jacket and tie and opened his shirt to the waist. The man extended a hand which Bodie shook.

'Name's Al,' said the American. 'That's all the name we need. Glad to know you.' Al was chewing on the butt of a cigar. He looked, to Bodie, like the sort of punter who fancied himself as a player far more than his ability could match.

The second man was an effete, blond Englishman, a Ministry man probably. He had not even loosened his tie, and sat at the table drumming fingers impatiently on the cloth. He was introduced as Gregory and his handshake was limp, effete, and almost suggestive.

Tina came up with the drink, which Bodie gratefully took from her. His hand touched hers, and the touch was held, the gaze between them explicit, probably genuine on her part.

But Johnny Hollis's hand came down on Bodie's shoulder, at first in a friendly gesture, but a touch that quickly turned into an aggressive and painful squeeze. Tina turned on her heel and walked quickly back to the bar. Bodie watched the swivel of her full hips with deliberate rudeness, then turned his gaze to meet Hollis's cold, grey eyes. 'Tina only serves drinks,' said Hollis, a distinct edge to his voice. 'Please remember that, Mister Bodie.'

He ushered Bodie to one of the vacant chairs, and Bodie sat down, smoothed the cloth in front of him, smiled at the sour-faced Gregory, and said, 'When do we start?'

'As soon as we're all here,' said Hollis, and glanced as discreetly as possible at his watch. 'Ah ... I believe our fourth player has just arrived.'

Bodie could hear voices, a man's voice, and that of a woman. Hart appeared in the main body of the suite, and behind him walked the dapper form of Tefali Rahad, a tall, elegant blonde on his arm. That was Anna, Bodie knew, and he could immediately see why Doyle had been so wistful when they had talked on the phone earlier in the day.

Doyle was as confused as was Bodie as to exactly how Cowley's Operation Fix Rahad was scheduled to develop. He was glad to have had Doyle's side of things, but the greyness was still irritatingly complete.

Close up, Anna was very tasty indeed. She stood coyly in the entrance to the card room while Hollis brought Rahad over to meet the other players. 'Gentlemen, this is Mister Rahad. Mister Rahad, your challengers for the evening, all personally known to me –' Bodie grinned inwardly at the lie '– Al, that's all the name he wishes to use; Gregory. And this is Mister Bodie.'

Rahad nodded to each of them, then moved to sit down at the table, taking the seat opposite to Bodie. Tina came up with a tall glass of what looked like orange juice and placed it on a mat next to the Arab. Rahad touched her hand gently without looking at her, which was as well since Tina was looking at Bodie. Anna had moved into the suite, and was sitting, drink in hand, looking around her.

The American, Al, said bluntly, 'Come on, let's get on with it. Been here twenty minutes. Getting fidgety.'

'My sentiments exactly,' said Bodie, giving Rahad a coarse, insulting look.

Rahad smiled evenly. 'I apologise if I have delayed proceedings, gentlemen.'

Hollis stepped into the circle of light, and leaned on the table between Bodie and Gregory. 'All right, now listen to me. A couple of you, Bodie here, and Al, are new to this particular game. I would just like to point out that Lucho . . .' Lucho moved into the room as his name was mentioned. 'Lucho is here to see fair play. Any disputes, be very careful before you ask Lucho to mediate. The house rules are very simple. Aces high, and if there are any problems, I have the last say. The house will take ten per cent of every pot. Good luck to you, gentlemen.'

Hollis withdrew. Lucho stepped forward and broke the seal on the first pack of cards, dealing them round the table until the first ace landed opposite the American. Al took the pack, shuffled it expertly, then offered it to Bodie to cut. Bodie tapped the pack, staring all the time at Rahad, who was aware of the irritating, hostile scrutiny, but was managing to remain pleasantly aloof.

But Bodie had been programmed, and he started the sequence of his act.

'I'm surprised to see you here,' he said to Rahad.

Rahad's eyebrows flinched slightly, then he smiled. 'Have we met before Mister Brody?'

'No. Not that I know of. It's just that I was told they didn't allow any Coloureds in the game.'

Rahad's composure vanished for a split second, a frightening shadow passing across his face. He met Bodie's insolent stare evenly, and quickly regained himself. Smiling, he said, 'WE have the *oil,* Mister Brody. That makes us pure white.'

Gregory laughed politely. Al just scowled, tapped the cards impatiently on the table. But Bodie, by dint of his hostility, was holding up play.

'The name's Bodie,' he said to Rahad. 'Not Brody . . . *Bodie.*'

Rahad inclined his head in acknowledgement. 'And it is a name I shall remember.'

'Come to think of it,' Bodie persisted, 'I didn't think Arabs were allowed to play poker. Religious reasons, or something.'

Rahad raised his hands in a gesture of affirmation. 'Quite so, Mister Bodie. Nor do we drink alcohol.' He raised his glass of orange juice, toasting Bodie's health. Then he glanced at Al. 'Let's play cards, Al. I'm quite in the mood to watch a man lose.'

As the game got underway, Johnny Hollis and Tina went into a second, small room, hidden from general sight in the suite. Here, in semi darkness, were two TVs, each showing the game from a different angle. The concealed cameras were slightly elevated so that the cards could be seen as each player held up his hand to check it.

But the main point of the closed circuit TV was not to cheat, not to assist Hollis and his 'game's man', Gregory, to fraudulently take the biggest pots. The TV system was designed to watch the players themselves.

And tonight they were especially watching Bodie.

Hollis was not alone in this.

If he had taken the time to look out of his apartment window, if his eyesight had been sufficiently good to allow him to see details of the car parked some two hundred yards away, along the street, he would have seen a pair of intense, blue eyes watching him back.

Slumped in the driver's seat of his car, Ray Doyle had decided, off his own back, to keep an all night vigil outside the exclusive block of flats. He knew the danger Bodie was up against, and he knew Bodie was unarmed.

It seemed like a good thing to do, standing by . . . just in case something went wrong; just in case Cowley's plan threw up its first wrong move.

His radio bleeped and Doyle glanced at it sourly; he knew this would be Cowley. Picking up the R/T he signalled, 'Four five.'

'Alpha One,' said Cowley's voice. 'Where on earth are

you, four five?'

Doyle licked his lips, peered through the windscreen and up at the apartment where Bodie was playing cards. 'Er, keeping observation sir, outside the Hollis place.'

Cowley sounded distinctly irritable. 'Go home. I repeat, go home.'

'But I thought I'd . . .'

Cowley interrupted him angrily. 'Four five, you have your orders! Start up and get out of there. If anything goes wrong at the card table, you wouldn't know about it. And even if you did, you'd never get up there in time.'

Cowley was right, Doyle knew. It made no sense at all him sitting here like a dummy. If Bodie was mugged, shot, or even abducted, there was no way, short of his corpse being brought out down the front steps, that Doyle would find out about it immediately.

He had known Bodie a long time. They had worked some tough, and damn near suicidal capers together. So why was he so concerned now?

The operative word was *together*.

Right now, Bodie was playing the high stakes alone, and without the possibility of assistance. Doyle felt out of things; he felt a little alone; he didn't like the idea of working with another partner.

To Cowley, via the radio, he said, 'It's a bit strong, isn't it? Leaving him to . . .'

'He'll fend for himself very well indeed. Return to your apartment and confirm your return to Control. Out!' And the radio clicked into silence.

'Dammit,' said Doyle, and with a last glance to where Bodie was playing the table, he started up his car and drove home.

Bodie was in his element.

They had played poker for two hours and, though he couldn't be sure, he was almost totally convinced that the game was being played straight. He had won, he had lost; no pot had gone above two hundred pounds. Bodie was down by about four hundred.

Gregory was sharp, very sharp. He played cautiously, but

he bluffed well. He was practised with the cards, dealing smoothly, efficiently, rarely staying in the hand beyond the draw. Bodie had him marked as Hollis's man already. That was okay. Just so long as the cards came from the top of the pack, and not the bottom.

Al, the American, was a big bluffer, a hard player, and a worrying one. He had the classic poker face, talked, swore, smoked, sweated. It was impossible to read through this huge act, and Al was, at the present moment, well ahead of the game. He chortled hugely each time he won, and made great play of raking in the notes in the pot.

Rahad was the best, though. He was assessing the opposition, playing practically, intelligently, mixing his styles so that Bodie could never pin him down to any weakness, any obvious form of play. He won, he lost. Like Bodie he was behind on the game, the only place for an ultimate winner to be so early in the match.

In the shadows, responding to requests for lights, drinks, snacks, Lucho and Tina were silent, watching figures.

Bodie had been dealt three tens, and the draw had not increased the value of the hand. Al threw in when Bodie raised by fifty pounds. Gregory checked, and Rahad raised again. Bodie was convinced, this time, that Rahad was bluffing, but he couldn't read the Arab at all. He was trusting to intuition. So he raised the pot again, and with satisfaction watched as Gregory, without hesitation, threw in his cards. Rahad stared hard at Bodie, weighing him up, running back through the run of cards for the ten games previous or so. He would have known, unless his memory was very bad, that there were three or four possible runs in the pack, and Bodie had drawn two cards. It would be three, then. Three of a kind.

But how high?

Bodie stayed impassive, watching the Arab. Rahad finally called him, and grinned broadly as he laid down his own three queens to Bodie's three tens.

Bodie swore inside. He had been well and truly beaten that time, and he should have spotted the play. But then again, that was the nature of the game. It would swing back to him . . . provided Hollis let the game play on naturally.

Rahad raked in the pot. 'You were surprised we play poker, Mister Bodie,' he said sneeringly. 'You must be astonished that we are good at it too?'

'You're not that good,' said Bodie challengingly. 'You're too smug to be that good.'

Rahad didn't rise to that one, merely shrugged and made a sound of dismissal.

Unseen to Bodie, Hollis watched the game from the TV room. Tina came in and he put his arm around the girl, then ran his hand up and down the fullness of her hips. She wiggled her behind with pleasure and began to tickle Hollis's ear.

Hollis said, 'Go and tell Hart to give Gregory the sign. This game has gone on long enough. It's time to fix that bastard Bodie. Time to fix him good.'

Tina slipped from Hollis's clutch, and went into the lounge area, where Anna still sat reading, glancing occasionally at the games room, and yawning.

Hart caught Tina's eye, raised an eyebrow, and almost imperceptibly acknowledged her brief thumbs up. Bodie, who had been watching the activity around the card table with care, didn't fail to miss the brief little exchange.

It was coming, he knew that now.

The game – for him – was almost over.

Gregory was dealing. His hands were a blur as he skidded the cards across the green baize cloth to the players. Bodie left his cards face down until all five were dealt. Al picked his up as they came one by one, scrutinising them closely, then laying them face down again, dividing them neatly into one group of two and one group of three.

He grinned at Rahad who had watched this little manoeuvre. Which group would he discard? That was Al's favourite tease, and it was the most excruciating weakness in his game. He couldn't resist that silly tease – the Texas tease he called it – and although he had *always* won the hand where he had played it, he was inevitably going to lose badly before too long.

Bodie picked up his cards and felt his heart miss a beat.

70

Then he remembered that this was almost certainly the fall game.

He stared at the three Kings in his hand and wished almost fervently that this was a straight hand. But regrettably it was not . . . even though he had to play it for keeps.

'I believe it's up to you, Mister Bodie,' said Gregory in his effete English accent.

This is it!

Bodie leaned forward and pushed a small stack of bank notes into the middle of the table. 'I'll open for four hundred,' he said, and looked hard at Rahad.

Rahad thought just briefly, watching as Al, sitting next to Bodie, threw in his hand. 'That's already too rich for my blood.'

Rahad pushed four hundred pounds into the middle. Gregory did the same, then looked at Bodie, who skated two cards back to the dealer and picked up the two replacements.

He found himself looking at a hand of four Kings. The biggest hand he'd ever held in his life, in a game of this calibre.

Damn, he thought.

Rahad also took two. Gregory took three, and Bodie smiled at that.

Bodie raised the pot by two hundred pounds, then smiled at Rahad who, with an almost contemptuous look raised that by five hundred. Gregory did a quick assessment of the two players, and . . .

With a brief look at his cards . . .

Began to play the big stake that Bodie knew was coming. He raised the pot by nine hundred pounds. Rahad glanced at him, then looked at Bodie, then began some very hard thinking.

Bodie saw the pot, pushing nine hundred into the centre. Rahad did likewise, clearly not too happy about it, but still confused as to why this game had suddenly gone so hard.

Al rose from the table and went to fetch a drink. Gregory fanned his cards, looked at Bodie, looked at Rahad, closed the fan and smiled. 'Well, gentlemen, I think I must raise again. To the tune of fifteen hundred pounds.'

Al, from the bar, made the sound of a man in agony. How

much he would have liked to have been in on this one. It just hadn't suited his game plan to bluff at this time.

Bodie checked his four, sweet Kings. 'Well, Mister Gregory. I think I'll just have to stay along for a while.'

Rahad closed his hand and passed it tidily to Gregory, who placed it on the table. Rahad said, 'That's just a little steep for me. Good luck gentlemen.' But he stayed at the table, watching.

Gregory said, 'To me again. Well, I think a thousand pounds is in order at this time. That's a thousand to you, Mister Bodie. A thousand to see what I've got.'

'Seems to me, Mister Gregory,' said Bodie happily, that you've been doing all the raising. And that just isn't democratic. I'll stay in, your thousand, and a thousand more.'

Bodie pushed the money into the centre. As he leaned back he could hardly resist looking at Gregory's face, but he sensed the man looking at the area of table just before Bodie, where there was very little left in the way of table stake.

Bodie was practically cleaned out. If Gregory raised him, then it was lose . . . or play against a marker.

Gregory raised the bet, of course. 'I'll stay along,' he said, matching Bodie's thousand. 'And I'll raise . . . to the tune of two thousand more. What do you say to that, Mister Bodie?'

Al came and sat down again, his pudgy hand clutching a tall glass, with a double scotch inside it. He stared at Bodie, and he hardly breathed.

The room was electrically tense, silent. The pressure was tremendous.

Bodie didn't even look at his hand. He signalled for Hart, who moved rapidly across and leaned down. Bodie said, 'Will Mister Hollis take my marker?'

'How much?' asked Hart.

'Enough to stay in. And raise.'

Hart said quietly, almost disbelievingly, 'Have you got that kind of money?'

'I can get it,' said Bodie without expression in his voice. After a moment's contemplation, Hart said, 'Very well, Mister Bodie, we will accept your marker for . . ?'

'Four thousand.'

Hart scribbled on a pad of paper. Bodie signed his name. Then he turned to Gregory. 'Good. So now, Mister Gregory, to see me it's going to cost you two grand.'

Gregory grinned, glanced at Hart. 'Oh, but I don't want to *see* you, Mister Bodie. Not yet. I'll stay, and I'll raise you. By two thousand pounds.'

Al gasped. Rahad chuckled, sat back in his chair and sipped orange juice, his eyes never leaving Bodie's face. Bodie looked duly uncomfortable, fidgeted a little, then glanced at Hart, who nodded.

'How much?'

'Enough to see him,' said Bodie, sounding like a man defeated. Hart added the amount to the marker, Bodie signed, and then turned to Gregory.

'Let's see what you've got.'

Gregory smiled and nodded his head, looking at his hand. 'Two pairs, Mister Bodie. Two very nice pairs . . .' he laid down his cards, adding, 'Of matching Aces.'

Rahad laughed, shaking his head as Bodie's four Kings fell from Bodie's hands, Bodie looking shocked . . . shattered.

Al, the American, merely shook his head, making a sound like, 'Ay-yi-yi-yi.'

After a pregnant moment's silence, Bodie stood up at the table, staring accusingly at Gregory. 'You dealt that hand . . .'

'My dear Mister Bodie,' said the impeccable Gregory, 'What on earth can you be suggesting. . . ?'

Bodie banged the table with his fist, his face flushing, his eyes wide and angry. The money, and Rahad's drink, jumped slightly.

Before Bodie could speak, however, a hand rested gently, then more firmly, on his shoulder. He glanced round to see Hart standing there, looking almost sorrowful.

'Mister Bodie. Could you spare a moment? Mister Hollis would like to talk to you. To make arrangements for the payment of your marker.' He said it quietly, but menacingly.

Bodie straightened up, glanced back at the other players, then touched his hand to his forehead – a gesture of farewell.

'Thank you for the game, gentlemen,' he said, and Rahad waved back with his fingers, still highly amused by Bodie's total defeat.

Hart led Bodie through the lounge, where Anna watched him curiously, but smiled when he winked at her, and into the small back room where Hollis, Tina and the ape called Lucho were waiting for him. Hollis was seated on the edge of a small desk, looking down at the paper marker for six thousand pounds that Bodie had signed. He looked up pleasantly as Bodie was ushered in. Lucho stood to one side, hands folded across his groin, eyes never leaving Bodie's fidgety, nervous form.

Bodie undid his tie and collar button, and shuffled from foot to foot, glancing round at Hart, then back at Hollis.

Hollis said, evenly, 'This is a very high marker. You're into me for a good bit of money.'

Sharply, Bodie said, 'Why don't you get Gregory in here too. There's a few things you ought to ask him.'

Hollis smiled. 'What exactly does that mean?'

With a glance at the huge man standing so close to him, Bodie pressed ahead, 'I think it was a set up. The classic lead on play.'

'Surely, Mister Bodie,' Hollis was oozing reasonableness, 'Surely you're not suggesting that we run a crooked game here . . . ?'

As he spoke he glanced at Lucho and nodded. Bodie caught that signal and half turned his face to the heavy man, but Lucho acted with surprising speed. He punched Bodie hard in the stomach. Bodie doubled, clutching his gut, then yelled and staggered as a second blow caught him. Bodie fell to his knees, then further forward, leaning on one hand, waiting for the connection of Lucho's foot with his side. When the blow came it was softer than he'd expected, but it still sent him sprawling, gasping for breath.

Lucho reached down and his two brawny, hairy hands grabbed Bodie's lapels, and jerked him to his feet. Hollis stood in front of him, shaking his head. 'I'm sure you wouldn't be crazy enough to accuse us of not running a straight game.'

Bodie shook his head, glumly. It was not a hard gesture of

defeat to act: he'd have given practically anything, at that precise moment, to have taken both Hollis and Lucho apart. He knew he could have done it.

Damn Cowley! Tying my hands like this!

Hollis had picked up the marker again, and was staring at it. 'Going to take you a long time to pay this off. Lot of money.'

'I'll pay it,' muttered Bodie, still holding his stomach where the pain seemed to recur in waves from the growing bruise.

'Plus our twenty-five per cent interest,' Hollis went on. 'That makes a big difference. Yes, Mister Bodie. This marker is going to hang round your neck for a very, very long time. Like . . . ' he grinned pointedly as he stared at the miserable CI5 man. 'Like forever.'

'I'll *pay* it,' Bodie stated bluntly, then leaned back against the wall, still quite breathless.

Hollis sneered. 'You can't pay this off, Bodie; don't try and kid me. You're not in so good with that Terringham girl, now. You've pawned everything of value that you possess. But I like you, Bodie. I really do.' Hollis walked across to him, and took Bodie's jaw in his hand, lifting Bodie's face so that their eyes met. 'Yes. I like you. So I'm going to give you a break. A chance to pay this marker off . . . '

Bodie looked interested. Hollis let him go, stepped back and folded his arms, looking as if he was amused as he stared at Bodie, watching the man try to comprehend what could possibly be coming next.

'You're talking about . . . ' Bodie hesitated, frowning. 'Not money . . . what then? Kill someone?'

Hollis laughed. 'My dear Bodie, nothing so Hollywood.' He sounded like Gregory, putting on a forced, cultured accent. Moments later he returned to his London 'common'. 'For Christ's sake . . . *kill* someone.' Next to him, Lucho laughed, as if it was possible that his surviving brain cells had grasped some joke or other. Hollis went on, 'Information, Bodie. That's all. Just information.'

'And what exactly can I supply you with? What makes you think I know anything of interest to you.'

Hollis chuckled. 'I expect you hear things . . . in the course of your work, that is. Your work for . . .' exchanging a glance with Hart, 'For CI5?'

Bodie's eyes widened, and he lurched up from the wall, looking like he might attack Hollis. Lucho stepped in, slapped him round the face, sending him back into a leaning position.

'How the hell d'you know that?' shouted Bodie, then cradled his face, thinking wryly that Ray Doyle had got off quite lightly with his single blow to the lower left jaw. Bodie was taking punishment!

'We know all about you, Mister Bodie. Your partner is called Ray Doyle. Your boss is George Cowley. You've been working for CI5 for several years, and before that you were a soldier . . . and a mercenary . . . and more besides. The question is . . .' he stepped forward and waved the marker under Bodie's nose. 'The question is, do your bosses know about your gambling? And what would they say, eh? What would they say if they knew you were into me for this kind of money?'

Bodie looked horrified. He couldn't make his face drain of blood, but he acted out the part of a man stricken by a sudden terrifying realisation. But he quickly grew angry again, murmuring, 'Doyle, Jesus, Ray Doyle's done this! He's the only one who knew!'

Hollis said, 'It's a squeeze play, Bodie. And you're the nut in the middle. I tell you, it'd be far easier to go along with me . . .'

'That's your idea of a break, is it? Give information from CI5?'

Hollis grinned. 'There's another kind of break . . .'

And Hart added, 'That's where we start with your fingers and work up to your neck.'

Grinning like an ape. Lucho added. 'Slowly. Very slowly.' To emphasise his point he cracked his knuckles; the sound was like a branch being torn off a tree.

'What do you say, Mister Bodie?' prompted Hollis.

Bodie said, 'What can I say, *Mister* Hollis? I have no choice.'

'Very sensible,' said Hollis.

'There's just one little thing, though,' added Bodie. 'One tiny addition to my marker . . .'

Hollis frowned. Hart backed away, sensing Bodie's meaning. Lucho, the ape, just stood there, looking stupid, until Bodie's right hook – a real Bodie special – caught him and he collapsed to his knees, eyes open and staring, but dead to the world.

Chapter Six

Although Tefali Rahad had expected the game of poker to last well into the early morning, the crushing defeat of the man, Bodie, essentially finished the sport for the night. The American was unnerved by the shock play, and made his excuses to leave, and Rahad didn't feel that a game with one soft-mannered Englishman was up to much.

He thanked Hollis for a pleasant evening's entertainment, fetched Anna, and made to leave.

As they walked to the door, he glanced back to see Bodie's form being half carried, half walked from the room at the far end of the lounge. Lucho was massaging his own brawny knuckles, looking unhappy, but slightly triumphant.

Rahad guessed that Bodie had not been too happy with the arrangements to pay his marker. He couldn't blame him. It just seemed pointless to argue with the muscle in the shape of a man like Lucho. Quite pointless.

So Rahad and Anna returned to the Embassy, where they finished the champagne that Rahad had bought in for the girl, talked a little, then went through to Rahad's small, soft-lit bedroom.

Imagining Anna to be inexperienced, Rahad's love-making was gentle, to begin with, and quite tasteful. But as his passion grew, so his dominance took over, and he began to treat Anna like one of the whores who came to service him. He seemed to get a kick out of Anna's acted discomfort, her loudly voiced shock, her strangled cries of enjoyment.

Just after midnight, however, their intimacy was rudely interrupted by a loud knock on the door. Rahad ignored it for a while, but whoever was there was persistent, and with a great sigh of irritation, and a softly expressed apology, Rahad left the bedroom, pulling on his bath-robe.

Anna heard Rahad call through, 'Who is it? I'm busy.'

The voice that answered was that of a man, who announced that he was 'Colonel Kaffir. I have to see you right away.'

Rahad was clearly disturbed by Kaffir's arrival. He told the man to wait, returned to the bedroom, kissed Anna lightly. 'I have to discuss business for a few minutes. I am most sincerely sorry. I shan't be long.' And he closed the bedroom door very deliberately behind him as he left.

Anna slipped out of the bed and went to the door, pressing her face against the wood and listening. Although Rahad spoke softly he was so upset by Kaffir's message that his voice kept rising. She was able to pick up a great deal.

'I have made it clear,' Rahad said irritably. 'I do not want to be involved in another execution for a while. I am still watched. It is too risky.'

Kaffir said, 'This is a matter of very great urgency. Word came through only tonight, and the death of the man is essential. There is no other who can accomplish it, Rahad. The instructions are specific. It is to be you.'

'This is madness,' Rahad complained. 'Achmed Rajavi knew I was coming. Special Branch have a shadow on me. CI5 are probably sniffing around. I have explained this at length. If I take the Faisid assignment it is quite likely to be the last thing I ever do. Are they now so contemptuous of my skills that they are prepared to abandon me?'

'Faisid is not Rajavi,' murmured the other man. 'The importance of killing Faisid is to create diplomatic embarrassment. An embarrassment that we will benefit from in a very rich way. I am sorry, Rahad. It must be done, and you must do it.'

'Madness,' repeated Rahad. But Anna heard the door to the suite close. She walked quickly back to the bed and lay upon it, and when Rahad returned to the room she extended her arms invitingly.

Rahad was sour faced, obviously upset, but he stripped off the robe and smiled as he lay down with Anna. 'You look like you need a little diplomatic soothing,' she said and Rahad laughed.

'That I do, my dear. A *great* deal of soothing.'

* * *

Ray Doyle had been up since six, unable to sleep comfortably, and consequently quite wrecked. He wandered about his apartment, holding one cup of coffee after another, trying to shake some alertness into his head.

Bodie rang him about seven, sounding thick-lipped and pained. 'You got away with it, then?' said Doyle.

'Just,' said Bodie. 'Got a couple of hands I didn't expect, that's all.'

Doyle chuckled. 'I bet you threw your fist first, though.'

At the other end of the line Bodie made a sound like a man wincing with pain. 'I thought he was down for the count. Bloody near broke my hand, and he just got up again and slammed me.'

'How much you into them for?'

'Six grand,' said Bodie, and Doyle whistled. 'But they took the hook. Information, eyes and ears open around CI5, and in twenty-five years they'll pat me on the head and tear up the marker.'

'Nice one, Bodie. See you later.'

'Uh-uh,' groaned Bodie. 'I'm not moving for a day. And if Cowley thinks I'm getting soft . . . for once I might agree with him.'

As Doyle hung up the phone, peering at his empty cup and thinking about a fifth coffee, the doorbell went. He glanced at his watch, frowning. Who the hell could that be?

When he opened the door he was startled, although not displeased, to see Anna standing there. She looked slightly dishevelled, very tired. 'I need a coffee,' she said. 'Any chance?'

'Yes, of course.' Doyle stood back to let her pass, looked out into the corridor before closing the door. 'What happened? You look like you've been walking all night.'

Anna flopped down into an armchair. 'Walking? You mean like on two feet? You must be joking. I've been horizontal so long I'm still feeling giddy standing up.'

Doyle chuckled, running a hand through his mop of unruly hair. 'Feel a bit like that myself. Couldn't sleep last night.'

'Didn't get a chance to.'

'Lot on my mind.' Doyle went into the kitchen. Anna

yawned wildly. 'Lot on my everything.'

She held her cup in two hands, sipped it, making sounds of great appreciation. 'I think I've got a champagne hangover,' she said. 'Really awful.' She winced as she spoke. Doyle thought of Bodie, another of Cowley's 'players' in great pain.

'Did you see the poker game?'

'Some of it.' She looked up at Doyle and smiled. 'Your man did well, though he got a bit aggressive at the end. They worked him over a fair bit.'

'Water off a duck's back. What happened to you, anyway? Why are you up so early?'

She leaned back, half closed her eyes. 'That's why I thought I'd better come round here first. He chucked me out at five-thirty this morning and rushed off somewhere. Well, not exactly rushed, but he'd made an appointment that he didn't want to keep, and he left the Embassy at crack of dawn.'

Doyle watched the girl thoughtfully. 'Any idea where he went?'

'I had to listen hard. It was about midnight, perhaps after. Rahad got a visitor, a tall, beefy looking Arab. I looked through the keyhole. I think his name was something like coffee. Colonel coffee?'

Doyle laughed. 'That's Colonel Kaffir. He's a big number in that Embassy's Military Intelligence.'

Anna was nodding her head almost too vigorously. 'That's it. Kaffir. Colonel Kaffir. Well ... you must remember, I was listening through the bedroom door, and they were speaking Arabic, but I could understand most of it ...'

Doyle was surprised. 'You speak Arabic too?'

'You have to, in my profession.' Anna smiled sweetly. 'Especially these days. A couple of years ago it was Japanese. It's amazing how quickly you pick up the lingo, and it always impresses the punter.'

Cutting in, sensing that Anna was tired enough to ramble off on any track at all, Doyle said. 'What did they say, Rahad and this Kaffir?'

The girl placed her cup down carefully, rubbed her bleary

eyes with the backs of her hands. 'Something about this morning. Rahad didn't want to do what Kaffir wants him to do, but there's a "diplomatic embarrassment" being planned. I get the feeling someone's going to be killed. I picked up a name: Faisid. That's all I could make out. There must be hundreds of people called Faisid, so I don't know if that's any sort of help at all . . . '

She stopped talking. Doyle had leapt out of his chair and was at the phone, frantically dialling.

Sir John Terringham, turned from the window of his office and stared at George Cowley. Cowley thought that he had never seen such anxiety on the normally placid man's features. Terringham was pale and drained, very, very concerned.

'We can't be sure it's *that* Faisid. And we can't be certain that Rahad is to assassinate the man . . . '

Cowley made a sound of exasperation, slapping his hands against his sides and walking across the room. 'Rahad doesn't get involved in anything *but* assassinations. They wouldn't ask him just to frighten the man. They certainly don't want Rahad to deliver Faisid's milk. No, Sir John. This *must* be an execution.'

Terringham breathed deeply, staring at the carpet. 'That would be a major political disaster. If it is *the* Faisid that Rahad has got in his sights.'

There was always that slight edge of doubt, Cowley knew. In the diplomatic and business world of the various Arab presences in England, there were five men with the name Faisid, all of them prominent, all of them possible targets for a killer like Rahad. Who was to know which among them was, or was not, an undercover agent, or a subversive of threatening nature to the ruling government of their home countries.

But Emura Faisid was no ordinary diplomat. In fact, he was no diplomat at all. He was an ex-minister in exile, granted the protection of the British Government. He was from a country bitterly opposed to the ruling regime in Rahad's home state . . . and if Rahad killed him, if Faisid died in any way *at all* that could be considered unnatural, the diplomatic consequences were almost unthinkable.

'It would be seen as a breach of trust by Her Majesty's Government. Faisid's supporters are legion, his family is all powerful, and almost certainly will return to power within a few months. Faisid will return triumphant, and our oil concessions from his country will remain in power. But if Faisid dies . . . ' Terringham shook his head. 'Oil, industry, construction . . . billions of pounds will be lost to us, and also our only real ally in a politically hostile area of the Middle East.'

'Who's watching him?' Cowley took a step forward again, but was uncomfortable with Terringham's mournful concern.

'Special Branch. Flying Squad. And CI5, I hope.'

Cowley reached for his coat. 'If there's to be an attack it sounds as if it will be today. I have a schedule of Faisid's movements and plans for the day. But we're watching *all* the possible targets, and our men are spread thin . . . '

Terringham closed on George Cowley. 'Don't let anything happen to the man. For God's sake, George, keep Faisid alive.'

Cowley picked up Ray Doyle and they drove to a rendezvous with members of the Special Branch, inside Regent's Park, in line of sight with the ornate mosque where Faisid was at prayer.

'From the mosque he'll walk home, and take lunch,' said Cowley, reading from the schedule. 'This afternoon, two appointments in Kensington, then home.'

'Active man,' observed Ray Doyle sardonically.

'Keeping his hand in, ready for the return to power.'

'Is that him?'

'Aye . . . '

Doyle leaned forward to peer out through the windscreen at the tall, elegantly dressed Arab who had just appeared from the mosque. He wore traditional, flowing clothes, not colourful, rather sombre, rather tasteful. He was a man in his fifties, white bearded and with the bearing of a man of wealth.

He began the leisurely walk across the park, clearly

83

enjoying the stillness of the day, the hint of warmth in the atmosphere.

Behind him, appearing from among the shrubbery, came a couple of joggers in bright blue track suits. They were heavy set men, with short hair, and as they jogged so a certain angular bulkiness in each of their breasts showed up the presence of handguns.

Faisid was unaware of their presence, and they, equally, seemed unaware of the Arab who strolled along so close to them. But their jogging was ridiculously slow, at times no more than on the spot, keeping Faisid in front of them.

Doyle laughed. 'Isn't that those Flying Squad boys ... Carter, and what's his name?'

'Reagan, aye. Not exactly well disguised.'

'It's so damned obvious. I can see Reagan's gun from here!'

Cowley shrugged. 'Well, if *we* can see it, maybe it'll put others off.'

Faisid had walked past the car, now, Carter and Reagan jogging breathlessly along behind, shadow boxing and wincing with effort. Doyle heard Carter complaining, 'Blimey, guv. Whose idea *was* this!'

'Get a grip and stop complainin',' snarled Reagan, glancing at Cowley as he trotted past. 'Mornin', sir, enjoying the weather?'

Cowley grinned and waved at him. Ray Doyle had detected something in Cowley's wily look. 'You don't mind, do you? That they're obvious, I mean. You're thinking what I'm thinking.'

'And what might that be, Doyle?'

'You *want* this to be a hit.'

Looking at his junior, Cowley's craggy features didn't quite crinkle into a smile, but there was a sparkle in his eyes that told Doyle that he was right. Cowley said, 'Appalling diplomatic and trade consequences if Faisid dies. But it would be a damned sight easier all round if we could cut Rahad down in the act.'

Doyle twisted in his seat, peered at the high buildings around the park, tall, white mansions, the homes of the very rich, the offices of the very classy. 'Trasker and his mob should have those buildings covered by now, so it won't be a long shot . . .'

Starting up the car, Cowley turned the vehicle round to face the receding form of Faisid; he eased the gear into first and let the car just crawl along the roadway.

'A long shot?' he said, 'No, that's not Rahad's style. Close quarters, a sure shot at point blank range. Or a knife, or a garrotte. He likes to make sure of his victims . . . and thank God this time we're ahead of the game.'

With a smirk, Doyle corrected. 'Thank God? Shouldn't you rather thank a hooker?'

With a grim little chuckle, Cowley said, 'Aye. She's done well for us.'

The two joggers veered off to the left, leaving Faisid alone again, but now under the invisible surveillance of a team securely hidden in the houses opposite the park. The joggers collapsed into a gasping heap, then sprawled out on their backs, labouring for breath.

Cowley urged the car forward a bit faster, keeping Faisid in sight. 'Hunter and his mob'll have him covered for the rest of the park. We'll see him safely home, then pick him up again this afternoon.'

Cowley drove swiftly out of the park, round the block, then parked close to Faisid's house, facing along the road to where Faisid strolled happily home after his devotions. Doyle studied house, street, windows, rooflines, and most especially the thin woodland that bordered the park at this point. Everything looked in order. Doyle could see the vague outlines of Special Branch men behind some of the windows adjacent to Faisid's temporary home. But the most exciting moment of the morning had been the delivery of cartons of milk and the thick Arabic newspaper that was thrust into the letterbox of the house.

There was no sign of Rahad, nor had there been.

'Are you sure he won't try a long shot?'

Cowley grunted. 'People tend to stick to their own style. Rahad has never used telescopic sights. I agree, there's always a first time, but it doesn't feel right to me. No, I think, if he's going to hit, he'll hit in the same way he dispatched Achmed Rajavi.'

If Doyle was silent it was not with agreement. Cowley didn't think the long shot felt right, but Doyle himself had a very irritating itch in his nose, on his back . . . he surveyed the street, the peaceful avenue, the ambling form of the deeply thoughtful Faisid, and something smelled *wrong* to him.

'I don't like it,' he said.

'What don't you like?' asked Cowley.

'Too quiet. It's wrong. Something's going to happen.'

Cowley chuckled. 'You've been watching too many films, Doyle. It's a well known fact that when things are quiet it's due to an absence of sound. It means nothing.'

'I feel an itch. I have a bad feeling . . . '

Responding to Doyle's obvious concern, Cowley paid him the respect of rolling down his window and leaning out, scrutinising the road before and behind, checking to make sure that there were no unanticipated heads, or gun barrels, poking or bobbing from windows and vantage points where there should have been nothing but pigeons.

'There's nothing to be seen,' he said, and Doyle smiled.

'Just tension, I expect. Sorry sir. But it would be nice if Rahad made his move now, us here, Hunter boxing him in at the other end. It would save us a lot of trouble.' He looked at Cowley, thinking of Cowley's complex game, the steps that they had made, the moves they had yet to make. 'Mind you,' he added, 'It would make all what we've done so far, all the setting up, me, Taylor, Bodie, Anna, all of that would just have been a waste of time . . . '

Cowley turned sharply on Doyle. 'No way is nailing Rahad a waste of time,' he said gruffly. 'Rahad's continued existence is a waste of life . . . '

Faisid trotted up the steps of his house and began to fumble for his key.

Cowley sighed. Doyle said, 'We're out of luck. False alarm. Sorry sir.'

'No, no . . . it was possible. And we *may* still have the wrong Faisid. Anna was quite right to mention this.'

'Yeah. Shame though.'

They didn't move, watching Faisid thoughtfully. Anna had said that Colonel Kaffir had wanted something done in the *morning*. But Rahad, already jumpy about being monitored by Special Branch, may have decided to strike later, and the monitoring of Faisid would continue.

'*Inside* the house . . . ?' said Doyle. 'I mean, it's not possible that . . . '

Cowley shook his head. 'Quite clean. And we have two men in there, standing by.'

Faisid had opened his door and was entering.

'What happens now?' said Doyle. 'Twenty-four hour watch?'

'More than that, I think. But for the moment, for us, I think we can leave Faisid in the safe hands of Special Branch.'

He started up the car again. Doyle stared down the road, then suddenly went pale, leaning forward, frowning.

'Wait a minute . . . Look at that!'

Cowley looked down the street, frowned in puzzlement, then realised what Doyle meant.

A paper boy was working his way up the road, pushing a trolley stuffed with papers, stopping at each house and working the bulky rags into the letter boxes.

But Faisid's paper had already been delivered!

Doyle said simply, in a voice filled with agony, 'The bloody paper!'

He leapt from the car, and streaked across the street, shouting, 'Don't touch the paper! Faisid, don't touch the paper!'

In horror he watched the paper withdrawn from the letter box, tugged inside the house.

Doyle veered to the right, eyes wide, mouth gaping, still half crying his warning.

The door blew outwards with a shattering explosion, a great thick, billow of smoke filling the air, windows shattered, and the dry crackle of flame reached Doyle's ears.

Through the smoke and the confusion, Doyle could just see part of a long, Arab robe.

Chapter Seven

Early in the evening of that same day, while the corridors of CI5 and Special Branch rang to the sound of furious recrimination, Tefali Rahad took Anna to his favourite restaurant in Knightsbridge, and dined and wined her in the most extravagant fashion.

He was well pleased with the way he had handled the Faisid project. At first reluctant to have anything to do with a further assassination, he had called in a 'marker' from one of his own countrymen, an ageing member of the diplomatic corps who had specialised in bomb-making, and who was glad to 'rig' Faisid's house in his special way.

Rahad had been nowhere near Regent's Park when Faisid had journeyed to meet his maker. And the boy who had delivered the paper, under the watchful eye of Special Branch, would not even be able to identify the older man. The bomb maker was also a master of disguise.

All highly satisfactory, really. Rahad would not be sent home in disgrace for having refused an assignment; rather, the word was that he was now highly in favour.

Hence the spontaneous, elegant and hugely costly celebration with the delicious Anna.

Anna ate slowly, but enthusiastically, sampling every exotic dish that she could, while Rahad informed her of what she was eating, what it meant, how it would be eaten in his home country: a fascinating 'restaurant tour' of his own world. Rahad himself ate very little, an unusual response after having achieved a kill.

He recognised what it was, though. Anticipation. Anticipation of the long night to come.

When they had finished eating they held hands across the table, talked intimately, then rather humorously, comparing the type of joke popular in the Middle East with that which could tickle the humour of an Englishman.

Rahad was eager for bed, and he paid the bill quickly, then escorted Anna out into the street, arm around her.

He looked to see where he had parked his sleek Mercedes, remembered it was some fifty yards towards Hyde Park, and began to saunter in that direction.

He suddenly stopped, appalled to see the figure of a man stooped inside his car. The man had managed to open the car door, and was busy rifling the interior for valuables.

'Hey!' shouted Rahad, and began to run up the street. Anna trotted behind him.

The man drew out of the car, and glanced anxiously towards Rahad. His boyish features grinned, curly hair blown by the light breeze. Then he turned and sprinted away.

Rahad gave chase for a few yards, but the man was too fast for him. Ray Doyle was too fast for most people.

Back at his car, Rahad drew out his briefcase, opened it, then checked below the dashboard, finally shrugging.

'He took nothing. That was fortunate. What's the matter, Anna?'

Anna was staring after the thief, her face frowning. 'How extraordinary,' she said.

'Not at all,' reassured Rahad. 'These days car thieves are everywhere. I never carry anything of real value, but I had important papers in my case, and sometimes the vandals destroy what is useless to them.'

Anna shook her head, still worried. 'I don't think he was a car thief. No, I'm sure of it, Tefali. I know him . . . I've seen him, at one of mummy's parties . . . '

Rahad was intrigued; he looked back along the road, then took Anna's arm. 'You know him?'

'He was at a party just recently, he and another man, older, crinkled. A Scotsman. I can't remember his name.'

'A friend of the family?'

But Anna looked Rahad straight in the eye, and grimly shook her head. 'No. Not at all. He was from the secret service. I'm almost sure of it: he was from the department they call CI5.'

Rahad gasped, appalled. 'I thought they'd been called off. This is infuriating!'

'What does he want, Tefali? Why should he be breaking into your car?'

Rahad smiled, leaned across to kiss Anna gently. 'Don't worry about it, my dear. In the diplomatic service one is often subjected to unwanted and unwarranted surveillance. CI5 have been watching me for two weeks, ever since one of our Embassy staff died under suspicious circumstances.'

Anna appeared to understand. 'And they suspect you?'

'They suspect us all,' Rahad lied fluently. 'But the watching is infuriating.'

He drove Anna back to the Embassy, and while she got prepared for bed, Rahad phoned through to the only person that he could think of who might be able to help him.

He called Johnny Hollis.

'What can I do for you, Mister Rahad.'

'You once told me that if I needed . . . personal help, one might say, that for a price you would do what you could.'

Hollis's voice sounded genuine as he said, 'I said it, Mister Rahad, and I meant it. What trouble are you in?'

'Surveillance trouble. Our own Intelligence Service monitors MI5 and the Special Branch. But there is another department that are a mystery to us. And I need to know what exactly they have on me, and why exactly they are following me.'

'Sounds . . . not easy. It depends. Which department?'

'CI5. Do you know of it?'

Whatever Rahad had expected by way of reaction from Hollis, he hadn't expected the sound of laughter. He took the receiver away from his ear and waited, puzzled. There was a sudden, abrupt silence at the other end of the line.

'Something is funny, Mister Hollis?'

'I'm sorry,' said Hollis. 'No, not funny. Just nicely, almost ideally coincidental. So you're having trouble with CI5. Well, I think I can help you, Mister Rahad.'

'You can? I'm delighted.'

'Come over tomorrow. I'll have something for you. But it'll cost you, and it'll cost you plenty.'

Rahad sneered at the mental image of Hollis. 'I fully understand, Mister Hollis. You will be well paid, have no worries on that score.'

The following day, Rahad drove the short distance to Hollis's suite of rooms, and was ushered in by Martin Hart. Hollis was delighted to see the Arab, almost seemed to be excited by something. Dressed in dark suit, his toupee properly positioned for a change, he took Rahad by the arm (something Rahad hated) and led the man to the bar, where Tina had made him up a fruit cocktail.

Rahad refused the drink coldly, but Hollis was not put out by that.

'You did the right thing calling me,' the mobster enthused. 'I said I would help, and I got onto it right away. It took me . . . ' he waved his hand slightly, 'A little time. It took me a little trouble. It cost me a lot of money.'

'But you *can* help. With CI5. You can get a man in to check their records?'

'I can do all that and more. You've come to the right man, Mister Rahad. I deliver the goods.'

Rahad grew impatient with Hollis's procrastination. What was Hollis up to? The man was grinning like an ape; he clearly had something extra up his sleeve, something that would surprise Rahad.

'Goods I don't need. Information on CI5 I do.'

'You're going to get a lot better than that.' Hollis stepped forward, looked closely at the Arab. 'I hold a marker that belongs to a CI5 operative. It's a big marker. The man is in big trouble. He's mine, Mister Rahad, mine to operate in any way that I want.'

Rahad was overwhelmed. He had never thought he could be so lucky!

'Just think,' Hollis persisted. 'Your own man on the inside. Your own man feeding information to you, doctoring reports, keeping your name clean. That has got to be worth forty thousand, hasn't it?'

Rahad came down to earth with a bump. 'Forty thousand! That's far too much.'

But Hollis wagged a finger under Rahad's nose, smiling as he did so. 'Don't tell lies, Mister Rahad. I know how you Arabs operate. I know you have a slush fund available, dirty money, pay-off money. I know that fund runs into hundreds of thousands of pounds. It's all chicken feed to you oil-rich bastards anyway. Forty thousand is peanuts. You can get it. You *will* get it. And just think how pleased your bosses will be with you.' He turned from Rahad, winking at Hart who stood in the doorway. 'A pet boy in the heart of the English secret service. They'll probably make you a general, or something.'

Irritating though Hollis's condescension was to Rahad, he couldn't help agreeing with the mobster. To get a man inside CI5 would be a terrific boon. It might *well* result in his promotion. 'Very well,' he said. 'I agree the price. Let me see the goods.'

Hollis grinned broadly, nodded at Hart who left the room. 'I knew we could do business. And very good business too. Here's your man, Mister Rahad. You already know each other, I believe.'

Rahad gaped as Bodie, looking mean and angry, stepped into the room.

'You!' said the Arab. 'You in CI5?'

Ignoring him, Bodie scowled at Hollis. 'What's going on? What d'you want to see me about?'

Hollis slapped him on the arm, led him across the room to stand before Rahad. 'You're a negotiable asset, Mister Bodie.' He handed Rahad the marker from Bodie's poker game. And I just sold you. You belong to Mister Rahad, now.'

'Bugger that!' said Bodie viciously. 'No bloody Arab is going to pull my strings.'

Lucho took a step forward, cracking his knuckles. Bodie didn't look at the towering form of the heavy, but his eyes lowered slightly as he realised he was in a corner.

Rahad shrugged, then smiled. 'It doesn't please me either Bodie. Although in one way it does. Your humiliation is my triumph. I enjoy that. But now you are working for me . . .' he waved the piece of paper. 'Until I agree that this is paid off.'

Bodie wiped a hand across his mouth, looking hard at the Arab, weighing the whole situation up. 'I'll not kill,' he said eventually, and Rahad chuckled. 'I won't be asking you to. Your job is much simpler. And to me, quite essential!' He turned to Hollis. 'I believe I *will* have that drink now. And one for Mister Bodie. He looks a little pale.'

So it was all working like clockwork; Rahad was rising to the bait, and the bait was juicy and irresistible; and the hook inside the bait was sharp and vicious, and it would snare Rahad with speed and finality.

Bodie made his way wearily up to Doyle's place. Weary because at last he could stop the sort of acting that most men won Oscars for. From now on his job was straight 'spy'. He could act himself; for all he needed to do, henceforth, was lie through his teeth.

And Bodie knew all about lying.

Perhaps it was relief that made him tired, relief that the tricky, complicated plan that Cowley had devised had, after all, worked out. So much had depended on Bodie acting a role with conviction, and Bodie had been nervous that he himself would let the game down. But he hadn't and now all the acting was up to Ray Doyle.

Doyle's turn in the frying pan. And about time.

What Bodie needed now were the simple comforts of a chat with a friend, a stiff drink, a large, medium rare steak, and most of all: a woman. The meal and the girl he had fixed up for later that evening.

For the drink and the chat he went to Ray Doyle's.

Doyle grinned as he opened the door, blue eyes flashing cheekily. 'Sorry ... you should be using the slave's entrance ...'

'It's going to be jokes, is it?' said Bodie dryly, pushing past and into the flat.

Doyle closed the door, shaking his head at Bodie. 'And *will* you be careful dragging your chains across my carpet!'

Bodie flopped down in a chair. 'Very funny. Ha ha. And tell me, Raymond, how's the hooker trade? Are you still pimping?'

Doyle looked wistful. 'That Anna's a lovely bit of crumpet. Really fancy that.'

'Out of your class,' said Bodie. 'And out of your price range. Whose idea was this, anyway?'

Simultaneously they said, with a chuckle, 'Yours!'

Doyle shook his head. 'No, it must have been Cowley's.'

'Which means it might work. Working all right so far. Trickiest bit to come.'

Doyle agreed with that. 'Very tricky. Listen, I'd offer you a drink, but . . .'

Bodie frowned. 'But what?'

'Well, do you think Mister Rahad would mind? I mean, seeing as how you belong to him, and how jealous those Arabs can be . . .'

He laughed at the expression of irritation on Bodie's face. 'Offer me a drink, Doyle, before I offer you my fist.'

Ray Doyle went to the drinks cabinet and poured two large slugs of scotch. 'Can it work, I ask myself. Can it really work?'

Taking his glass, and raising it to Doyle's health, Bodie said, 'Ask me tomorrow. I meet Rahad tomorrow, the boy bowing to the Master, and that's when I toss the baited hook.'

'Here's to a good cast,' said Doyle, and added with a smirk, 'Make sure you hook him right in the sheep's eyeballs.'

Rahad loved watching the way Anna rode. Her slim, curvacious body moved rhythmically up and down in the saddle, horse and rider one single, elegant unit of power and erotic motion.

Rahad cantered Sultan behind the girl. The park was empty, it being the mid-morning hour. It was colder today, a brisk wind fresh on the face, a hint of autumn in the air.

From the corner of his eye, Rahad saw the movement in the bushes on the left side of the riding track. He peered hard at the figure, trying to discern who . . . or what . . . it might have been. As he studied the foliage, Anna cantered on ahead, and Rahad was glad of that. Out of danger.

His heart beat a little faster. His head became clear. He knew that there were a limited number of deaths available to him, and that the sudden, explosive end at the hands of an assassin was highly probable. If he was to be killed now – and he had no gun on him with which to defend himself – he didn't want Anna in the line of fire.

But his sudden tension was unnecessary.

It was Bodie who stepped out of the bushes, raising his hand like a traffic cop to signal attention.

Rahad reined Sultan in and the horse whickered and snorted, and reached its head down to gently crop the fine cut grass of the park. Anna sensed that Rahad had slowed to a stop and turned Snoopy, reined the horse in and began to jog back along the track.

'Be with you in a moment, my dear.' Rahad called out, and Anna nodded to show she understood. She rested her horse, leaning down to pat its neck, allowing it to graze for a few minutes.

'Here?' said Rahad to Bodie, as Bodie walked up to the horse, taking the bridle in his hand. 'It's too public. If we're seen together . . .'

'Relax,' said Bodie. 'There's no-one around. Besides, you're as clean as a nun's mind.'

Grinning, Rahad slid out of the saddle, removed Bodie's hand from the bridle, and said, 'That's a matter for conjecture. What did you find out?'

Bodie said, 'All surveillance was pulled off you, shortly after you complained to Sir John Terringham. The reason given was "to avoid a diplomatic incident". You must swing some weight for Her Majesty's white collar boys to actually do what you asked.'

Rahad was obviously pleased. 'That's very good news indeed. Very good news.'

'Are you ready for the bad?' Bodie looked like a man relishing what he was about to inflict upon Rahad: pain, hurt, disaster . . .

'Go on . . . the bad news.'

Grinning, Bodie said, 'You're on record somewhere . . . extolling the virtues of Muslim womanhood . . . and knocking her Western sister.'

Rahad frowned. 'I'm on record in many places. Purity and honour are among our great traditions; the preservation of that purity and honour among our women is essential if our country is to set its example to the world.'

'Very noble,' said Bodie, and looked round at Anna. 'But speaking of *knocking* western women . . . I think you may have got the wrong end of the stick . . .'

If Rahad was puzzled for a moment, he quickly grasped the slang meaning of the word. 'I see what you mean. But why should that be of importance. When in Rome . . . or in *London* . . . ? We all do it. We all exploit and enjoy the West, even though we disapprove of it. Nothing filters home.' He smiled. 'Our "free press" sees to that . . . one's minor indiscretions are expected, tolerated, necessary . . . and they all remain anonymous.'

The horse reared its head up, tried to pull away, and Rahad calmed the beast, stroking its nose, talking calmly to the animal. When it was still again he looked back at Bodie.

Bodie said, 'That's a key word. Anonymous. You don't get my meaning, do you . . . well, let's make it clearer for you. Your lady friend,' he jerked his thumb towards Anna. 'You never introduced me. What's her name?'

Slightly puzzled, sensing that Bodie was hiding something of significance from him, Rahad said cautiously, 'Anna Jones.'

Bodie reacted with mild surprise. 'Well, well. She even told you her real name. That's very cool, although it makes you out to be an even bigger schmuck than I thought. Oh sorry, you're an Arab aren't you. Schmuck is probably inappropriate.' Rahad said nothing, just stared at Bodie, although every few moments he cast a nervous, worried glance at Anna. Anna was getting impatient, staring back along the track at the quiet conversation going on between the two men.

'Explain more,' said Rahad. 'I've never heard of Anna Jones. She's a well bred girl, but unremarkable in any way except physically.'

'Anna *Jones* . . .' said Bodie gleefully. *'Dame Sarah Jones?'*

Eyes widening, Rahad gasped. 'Sarah Jones? Not . . .'

'Right on, Rahad. Sarah Jones: bra-less, titular head of the Woman's-Lib-for-Muslim-Women-In-Our-Time movement. Climb down off your camels. Tear away your veils!' Bodie chuckled, his face a combination of hostility and delight. 'And you're shacking up with her daughter!'

After a few seconds, Rahad – staring at Anna Jones – said, 'I can't believe it. I just can't believe it. Has she tricked me? Or doesn't she know . . .'

Bodie realised that Anna might be threatened if Rahad thought she was deliberately setting him up. He would have to be told of that fact eventually, of course, but at a time when Anna was not around.

So Bodie said, 'Dame Sarah would manipulate her dead mother to score a point against the chauvinists. I didn't notice if Anna was in on the deal, but if I were you I'd send her packing ... and fast! Even your free press isn't free enough to suppress *this* little dalliance once it gets out. Which it will.'

Rahad turned bitter, disappointed eyes on Bodie. 'What are you telling me? What do you mean "which it will".'

'We're on to it. CI5 are on to it. And they're going to exploit it. They're going to use it against you, to break you, and to embarrass your Embassy.'

'When?'

'Soon,' said Bodie.

'Do you know how?' asked Rahad, still occasionally looking at Anna, but depressed, now, knowing that the fairy tale romance was ended.

'No, not off hand,' said Bodie, and then added slyly. 'But I can find out. For my marker returned.'

Rahad wasn't rising to that. 'Half your marker,' he said. 'Just half. I don't want to lose your services *quite* that quickly. Half your marker, Bodie, for you to find out how and when CI5 will try and destroy me.'

Thinking quickly, deciding there was nothing to be gained by bargaining (or so Rahad interpreted Bodie's hesitation) Bodie nodded. 'It's a deal.'

He turned away and walked along the track, back to the gates of the park. Rahad stared miserably at Anna Jones, then swung himself into the saddle. He rode slowly up to the girl, who watched him coming carefully, then smiled. She was aware of Bodie lurking in the bushes again, and knew that if Rahad tried to kill her he would have to deal with a forty-five Magnum first.

'Is everything all right?' she asked, and Rahad shook his head.

'Regrettably not. I have some urgent Embassy business and must take my leave. I shall call you when I can. That will be soon. Goodbye, Anna.'

And without kissing her, he reined Sultan around and began to canter from the park.

Behind him Anna wiped her forehead theatrically, glad that her job was finished, now, and that she could go back to simple hooking with simple minded punters.

Chapter Eight

Ray Doyle was just finishing his exercise routine, forty press-ups to end a vigorous twenty minute flexing and bending activity, when Bodie arrived back from his rendezvous with Rahad. Doyle had left the door open and Bodie crept in and gently, and firmly, pressed Doyle back to the carpet with his foot.

'I bet you'd love to, wouldn't you,' grunted Doyle.

'Love to what, put the boot in? Not with you, sunshine. Rahad maybe. Lucho definitely.'

Doyle jumped up and brushed himself down. 'Lucho? One of Hollis's heavies?'

Bodie stabbed a finger at his partner. 'Right. And he's mine, when we take 'em. Remember that.'

'Share and share alike . . . remember the CI5 motto.'

Bodie made an incoherent sound, then brightened. 'Fancy getting drunk?'

Doyle grinned. 'He took the bait?'

'Hook, line and fabrication. You should've seen his face. Right little picture. I reckon he was really stuck on our Anna. Sad, isn't it?'

'Heartbreaking,' said Doyle cynically. He grabbed his short, leather jacket. 'Was it drunk that you wanted to get? And would it be with a Marxist that you'd be wanting to pass the time, begorrah?'

Bodie grimaced at the appalling accent. 'You're about as Irish as chop suey,' he said. 'Who's this Marxist . . . Taylor?'

'Aye,' said Doyle. 'What you might call a little fart. We have to get him set up, now, ready for the final phase. Come on. Business and pleasure . . . manipulation and booze.'

They drove to Taylor's HQ in Shepherd's Bush, picking up two four-packs of John Smith's bitter on the way. Taylor's place was dingier and smellier than Doyle remembered from that night of his first 'contact'. The stairwell smelled of cats, the downstairs landing of stale food, the upstairs of both. Bodie gagged at the rotten odour. Doyle just shrugged it off. 'Reminds me of home,' he said. 'Cats everywhere. You get used to it.'

Taylor was disturbed by the sight of Bodie, but Doyle introduced him as a good mate, interested in coming along for the drink. They split three cans, supped, and spread out in the untidy publications room, feet on piles of magazines and lithoed sheets, eyes roaming the walls and bookcases taking in the plethora of heavy political literature.

'Why *did* you drop by,' Taylor asked at length. 'Come on, you're not fooling me, there's a reason.'

Doyle drained his beer can and reached for another. 'Right. You remember when we talked before? You gave me the distinct impression that your basic, simplified philosophy of life is that the end justifies the means. That's my philosophy too, by the way.'

Taylor shrugged. He was a pale-faced, drawn young man. His beard looked even wispier than Doyle remembered, but his blue eyes shone earnestly, intelligently. 'It *is* my philosophy, but so what? What're you driving at?'

Bodie sat quietly in the corner, drinking beer and staring at the youth. Doyle tried to act out the part of a totally reasonable man, someone who shared a deeper concern. He swallowed beer and stabbed a finger at Taylor. 'Money. You need money, don't you?'

'Yeah. Of course.'

'And if it goes to the right cause ... well, you'd do anything for it, wouldn't you?'

Taylor scratched his thin face, looking quizzically at the other man. 'Maybe,' he said. 'I still don't see ... '

'I might be able to put some loot your way. Quite a lot of cash. Very useful amount. Get a better printing room for a start ... '

Bodie snickered from the corner, nostrils wrinkling in disgust at the heavy aroma of stale everything. Taylor glanced at him, then ignored him again. 'What would we have to do?' he prompted Doyle.

Doyle sat back, shaking his head. 'No details for the moment. Just wanted to sound out your ideals ... your, er ... interest.'

'In money? I'm interested. We need cash bad, you know that.' He leaned forward conspiratorially, 'I'd be prepared to do quite lot. Law don't matter, as long as I know the consequences, and the chances. I mean, I could be your man if it's for a little . . . what can I say? A little demo-bending?'

'That's just what I have in mind,' said Doyle. 'I thought you'd understand. Okay, what I'm offering is ten grand. How does that sound?'

It sounded astonishing to Taylor. His eyes nearly popped, then he frowned, then laughed nervously looking from Doyle to Bodie. 'That's a lot of money . . . '

'Course it is,' said Doyle easily. 'Didn't I say I'd help out?'

'A *hell* of a lot of money,' went on Taylor, a hint of suspicion in his voice. 'For a demonstration.'

Bodie shifted in his uncomfortable corner chair. He'd been staring hard at the poster of the bespectacled blonde woman . . . the real Anna Jones, the real Woman's Freedom Fighter. He glanced across at the student and grinned. 'No ordinary demo, lad. A very special demo.'

Taylor comprehended. 'More of a power play?'

Bodie shrugged. 'I'd buy that. What do you say, can you get enough boys together?'

Ray Doyle grinned reassuringly at the younger man. 'Course he can, can't you Taylor?' He raised his beer can in a vague salute. 'He can get hard boys too . . . ready to hit something . . . in a good cause, naturally.'

Shuffling in his chair, Taylor seemed uneasy with Bodie's presence. He owed a favour to this Doyle character, but there was something not quite right about the two of them together: too hard, too certain, too positive. Doyle picked up the anxious feeling and said, 'Look, I'm vouching for my mate here. He's on our side too. Now how about the boys?'

Taylor shrugged his thin shoulders. 'No problem, as I said. You want them, for Saturday, right?'

'Right. Outside of a particular Embassy in Kensington, where a particular friend of ours will not be at all pleased to see you.'

'And the money? Cash. I want cash.' Taylor's eyes lit up greedily as he spoke. This was the best break he'd had for weeks.

Bodie said, dryly, 'It'll be cash on the nail, delivered the night before . . . '

Puzzled by that, Taylor turned to stare at him hard. 'The night before? That's an unusual set up . . . '

'Unusual situation,' said Doyle, and smiled as Taylor shrugged and said. 'It's a deal. Fine.'

Doyle and Bodie rose to their feet in a single action, exchanging a satisfied look between them. There was one other thing, though, and it might prove awkward.

'The cash . . . one thing about it,' Doyle said carefully. 'It's going to be in Swiss francs. Okay?'

Taylor wasn't bothered by that. 'The currency of corruption,' he said. 'Sure, why not. We can shift anything . . . provided it's money.'

Bodie went to meet Tefali Rahad at Nero's seedy club in Notting Hill.

Nero was behind the bar as Bodie entered, and gave the CI5 man a sympathetic, but friendly glance. 'Hear you ran true to form, man,' he called, and laughed. 'I'd stick to Monopoly if I were you.'

'History, Nero. All history now. I'm meeting . . . ah, there he is.'

Rahad sat at a table, looking hot, uncomfortable, and disgusted with the surroundings of the *Casino d'Or*. 'This is a filthy place,' he said by way of greeting as Bodie walked up to the table. The Arab wore dark glasses, and a dark, anonymous suit. His face was pinched, thin, angry. He was still very bitter about Anna's betrayal. Bodie intuited that Rahad had certain plans of his own in connection with the girl . . .

'Keep your voice down or you'll hurt Nero's feelings,' Bodie said loudly, with a touch of arrogant confidence about his voice. 'Anyway, you wanted to talk somewhere quiet. And this is as quiet a place as any I know.'

Waving a hand dismissively, as if to say never mind the excuses, Rahad asked quickly, 'Well? How does it look?'

'Looks bad. It's going to be nicely done. Nice and subtle. CI5 have got it well planned out.'

'My destruction, you mean . . . ' Rahad looked pale. His

eyes just visible through the shades, looked tired and worried. 'How will they achieve this masterstroke of diplomatic embarrassment?'

'There's going to be a demonstration outside your Embassy . . . the day after tomorrow.'

Unperturbed, Rahad waved a hand, shrugging at the same time, 'I know that. Some good, if effectively useless cause. It won't be the first time, nor the last. How should that worry me?'

Bodie sat down, leaned on the table and fixed Rahad with his smooth, arrogant gaze. 'Anna Jones will be there among them.' He smiled as Rahad reacted with surprise, perhaps even a little shock. 'Just her and a few of her loud-mouthed mother's group. The police'll break it up, of course, no trouble about that. But! And get this. The press will be covering the demonstration, right? And there's a TV interview fixed for later that same evening. Anna Jones will be quizzed on both channels, a nice, in-depth interview, questions about Muslim Women, women's rights . . . questions about your much publicised support for the Muslim Tradition, veils, humility, twenty paces behind the husband. Peak viewing . . . ' Bodie sat back, noticed that Nero was straining to catch every word as he pretended to wipe glasses at the bar. Rahad was cold, silent. He waited for Bodie to finish. 'Peak viewing, and that's when she'll break the good news.'

Rahad swore in his native tongue, his eyes closed, his lips moving even after the string of obvious obscenity had ceased. 'She will admit our love affair. She will say that I was her lover . . . it will destroy me, but it will also destroy herself . . . '

Smiling, satisfied, Bodie shook his head. 'No it won't. Why should it? She's for equality; she's for choice, and she's chosen the way to destroy you. She must hate your guts, Rahad. She must hate what you stand for even more.'

After a while, Rahad rose from the dirty table and paced around the club room, hands behind his back, body tense and stiff, a frustrated tiger, bursting to spring into action, but held by invisible ropes.

'She must not be allowed to talk,' he said at length. He didn't look at Bodie; he didn't look at anything; his mind would have been filled with a vision of Anna Jones, pumped full of lead, bleeding her life and her obsession away in some gutter, in some backstreet. 'I shall have to kill her. I shall do it soon . . .'

Bodie cut in angrily, 'That's right. Kill her and walk right into CI5's trap.' Although Rahad said nothing, he turned to face Bodie, peering down at the agent, perhaps thinking that when all this was over he would have to kill Bodie too. Bodie said, 'CI5 have affidavits, testimony, evidence, all against you. Anna spilled the lot. If she disappears, if you take her out by whatever means . . . *if she is assassinated* it'll be as good as a confession.'

The message sank in. Rahad's mouth pursed and he looked like a man in despair. Only the dark glasses maintained the vision of the cold blooded killer: but this man was on the run, now; in a hopeless mess; in need of advice, a friend, a way out.

In need of Bodie.

And Bodie would spring the trap. But he wanted Rahad himself to put a hand on the lever.

Rahad said, almost plaintively, 'What shall I do?'

'I don't know. There's got to be an answer. If I were you I'd keep your fingers crossed, hope you get lucky and that the demonstration gets violent . . .'

The Arab suddenly straightened up, peering into the distance, his lips parted in a half smile of realisation. Bodie said, 'No, too many cops. No chance. British cops can keep good order in a small demo like this. It might get violent, but not that violent . . .'

He was interrupted by Rahad, who breathed excitedly, 'No, no! That is the answer. That *is* the answer. The demonstration *can* get out of hand. Such things can be planned . . .'

Beautiful, thought Bodie. How nice to deal with an intelligent man who sees things as quickly as you. He wanted to smile, but he shook his head warningly. 'Outside an Embassy? *Your* Embassy? You've got to be kidding. Anyone lifts a *warning finger* they'll be inside a meat wagon so fast their feet won't touch the ground.'

Rahad would not be dissuaded. He was grinning now, visions of what might happen dancing in his head, pleasing the ruthlessness in him. An assassination by mob violence. What a challenge that would be to set up!

'It could happen,' he said to Bodie. 'Violence, and death . . . in a crowd . . . the demonstration will be covered by TV . . . no-one will suspect anything but crowd anger. A concerted rush by only European faces, by Westerners. Not an Arab face to be seen, no finger of suspicion to be pointed at our Embassy or *any* Embassy . . . '

'Damn!' said Bodie in mock admiration, his face showing the sudden realisation he felt that it just might work.

Rahad had warmed to his theme. 'The mob sways, chanting, angry . . . the police rush in to break it up . . . fighting, scuffling, blooded noses, and crushed underfoot, in a most *terrible* accident, the lovely Anna Jones. Dead. But these things happen, they *have* happened. And no one would point a finger anywhere except at the *causes*, at the *ideals*, the *reasons* for the demonstration in the first place. And they don't hang ideals. They don't behead reasons.'

Nero made a clattering noise behind the bar, and Rahad turned, realised that his voice had risen, then glanced back at Bodie and gave Bodie a thin, calculating smile. Bodie said, 'D'you know, it might work. It *could* work . . . '

'Of course it could.'

Bodie shook his head, 'But it would take too much organisation. You'd need a couple of dozen hard boys planted. And who do you know who . . . ?'

Interrupting him violently, Rahad stabbed a finger at Bodie and grinned, 'I know *you*! Who else do I need to know.' He patted his pocket, a hint at the marker that nestled there. 'You must know all the hard boys in London. Who else do I need? My trained ape can fix the whole thing.'

Bodie bristled slightly, but said, 'This'd be murder. No matter what it looked like, it'd be murder. That will cost.'

Rahad brushed that aside. 'I will meet all expenses . . . and I still hold your marker.'

'That damned marker.' Bodie held Rahad's gaze. 'I want the whole marker back. No arguments.'

'Yes. I agree.'

'And it's a thousand pounds a man, including me. I'll get ten. Including me. That's ten grand.'

Rahad just shrugged. 'That is nothing. You will have the money later this afternoon. We will meet back here after you have talked around your estimable colleagues. And by the day after tomorrow, Mister Bodie, we will both be off the hook.'

Bodie checked in with Cowley, confirming the arrangement with Rahad. Taylor had already organised his team to stir up the demonstration, and now all that needed to be done was to wait until after bank hours, then go back to the *Casino d'Or* and irritate Rahad intensely.

Bodie relaxed with a beer, a sandwich, and his radio. He missed his Hi-Fi, but would soon buy it back from the second hand shop.

Everything was going very smoothly. As he thought about that, Bodie shivered slightly, and his mouth went dry.

Everything going smoothly; too smoothly.

In a complex operation like this, something, somewhere would have to go wrong . . .

At four thirty he was back at Nero's club, facing the calm, less concerned figure of Tefali Rahad. Rahad had drawn the money out of his bank, and he opened the case to show Bodie the currency.

Ten thousand pounds in crisp, green English bank notes.

Bodie looked slightly abashed, closed the lid of the case and pushed it back to Rahad. 'Sorry mate. Wrong currency. I didn't realise it until it was too late, but they want Swiss francs.'

'What! Swiss francs . . . but why?'

'The currency of corruption. Sorry. They insist. Swiss francs or the deal is off . . .'

Rahad slammed his hand down on the bar top. 'This is absurd. I have the money in English notes . . .' he pushed the case back to Bodie. 'You will have to take it, get it changed.'

Bodie shook his head determinedly. 'Banks are closed, Rahad. These boys want paying off tonight. I can't get a bank to open for me. But you're not telling me you can't.

Your banks know which side their bread is buttered.'

Rahad sighed with irritation, then snatched back the case. 'Very well. I'll get the francs now. But *you* will be making the pay-off. You understand?'

'That's OK,' said Bodie. 'I'll be waiting where we agreed.'

Rahad stormed out of the Casino. Bodie grinned at Nero, who shook his head and said, 'I don't know a damn thing that's going on, mister. But it sounds to me like you're still gambling . . .'

'Can't resist playing games, Nero. And I can't stand Arabs. I'll soon have enough for another game stake.'

'Joy of joys,' sang Nero. 'More money for me and mine . . .'

Cowley took a detailed report along to the Foreign Office, for his appointment with Sir John Terringham. Terringham was still very much in the dark as to the nature of the connivance that Cowley had planned to 'embarrass' Rahad out of the country. He read the report through slowly, carefully, wonderingly.

When he had finished he threw the folder onto his desk, looked admiringly at Cowley, then said, 'By God, George. I'm glad you're on *our* side!'

Cowley grinned, pleased at the compliment, satisfied with his work, anxious for the work to be concluded. 'The last phase is being initiated now . . .'

'It all hangs together,' said Terringham. 'It makes sense in a convoluted sort of way. But will it work?'

Cowley looked away, the daylight sharpening his craggy features. 'It's got to . . . Doyle, Bodie . . . we've all of us put a great deal into it. There was one coincidence that we had to contrive: Rahad needing the CI5 man that Hollis had enrolled. If that had failed, the whole thing might not have worked. But Bodie acted well. We've all done our part.' Cowley picked up the photograph of Clare Terringham. 'Not to mention your own daughter.'

Terringham laughed, then frowned. 'Yes, she asked me some rather awkward questions about that chap of yours. Wondered if you'd been feeding him too much red meat?'

Cowley chuckled. 'You don't send a vegetarian to catch a jackal.'

With a wry smile, and a glance at Cowley that told of a sudden more serious meaning, Terringham said, 'Oh but you're wrong about the jackal, George. A rat is what *we're* after.'

Chapter Nine

The warehouse was a vast, black hangar. Disused for years, its crumbling concrete pillars seemed to hide shadowy, watching forms. Rubbish was strewn about its floor; moonlight lanced in through the shattered windows of its roof. Close by, the Thames rippled and splashed gently.

Rahad drove quietly to the rendezvous point with Bodie. This deserted warehouse was close to the place where Bodie would deliver the money to his mobsters. Rahad was uncomfortable coming so far from the gaudy safety of Kensington, but his anxiety to kill Anna Jones made him willing to go along with anything Bodie said.

He got out of the car, glancing at the lights across the river, then staring up at the dark, shadowy walls of the warehouse block. The doorway loomed and he stepped, suitcase in hand, into the interior.

A sound like something scurrying made him reach for his gun, but he recognised the vanishing form of a rat, and calmed himself.

Across the moonlit floor, emerging from an open entrance way at the far side of the storage area, a car without lights crunched on glass and purred into view. It stopped. There was a long moment's silence, then Rahad heard the door open, and saw Bodie emerge. 'Did you bring it?'

'I have it here,' called Rahad softly, and waved the case.

Bodie began to walk more swiftly towards him.

Suddenly, behind Bodie, there was the sound of car tyres screeching, light flickered off the walls of the warehouse, and the light grew stronger until two brilliant car head-lamps blinded Rahad for a second as the car tore into the deserted building.

Bodie ran for cover. Headlights still on the car stopped and a man jumped out, shouting Bodie's name. Rahad recognised the car thief, the one that Anna had claimed was from CI5.

Hollis had told Rahad that Bodie's partner was very, very uptight about Bodie's gambling. This must be the man, and he had come to interfere in Bodie's little deal with the Arab.

Bodie had started to run towards Rahad. The other man gave chase, still shouting. Rahad turned and fled back to his car, not failing to notice, however, that Bodie had pulled his gun.

The gunshot echoed deafeningly in the warehouse. The curly haired man arched backwards, then sprawled among the litter. His body twitched a couple of times, and then was still. Rahad took all of this in in a second, mind spinning. He had to ditch Bodie. He had to get away.

A second man had climbed from the car . . . Cowley!

Again a gun spoke, once, twice, the thunder of the discharge amplified in the enclosed space. Bodie ran after Rahad, spinning round, lurching, and clutching at his shoulder.

Rahad jumped into his car, turned the engine on, and fairly tore away, turning as tight a circle as he could manage so that he could go back the way he had come.

Cowley was running towards him, his figure lit up eerily by the headlights. Bodie was almost at Rahad's Mercedes, shouting. 'Wait for me. Wait!'

'Goodbye Mister Bodie,' said Rahad grimly, gunned the engine and drove Bodie down. Bodie hit the car, bounced and rolled off, and in his rear-view mirror Rahad could see the man's form lying motionless, spread-eagled . . . and twisted.

Rahad grinned.

He was untouchable. Even if Cowley had the suspicion that it might have been him in the car, they couldn't touch him. Diplomatic immunity. They would never prove that it was him driving, and without proof, and without access to the Embassy, Rahad knew that he was safe.

Cowley ran up to Bodie's still, silent form. He dropped to a crouch, and touched Bodie's shoulder. He still held his gun, and the acrid smell of powder was strong on the night breeze.

There was blood on Bodie's hand, and Cowley touched it gently. 'Oh Bodie . . . you did too much.'

Then he turned and called, 'Doyle! Quick!'

Ray Doyle leapt from where he lay, brushed himself down, then grinned; but as he grinned he saw Cowley crouched by his colleague, and he came running, fast, angry, momentarily panicked.

'Bodie!' he yelled, and reached to grip the man's shoulder. He'd been hit too hard by the car. God damn it! Something *had* to go wrong!

But then Bodie's eyes opened, his gaze shifting to look up at the anxious Doyle, who still held him by his shoulders. Bodie grinned hugely. 'Why Ray, I never knew you cared.'

Doyle released him in disgust. Bodie chuckled, sat up, and cradled his hand, which was bleeding very badly.

'You had me really going there, you bastard,' complained Doyle.

'I've been acting so much these past days I just forgot to turn off,' said Bodie. He climbed to his feet, and accepted the handkerchief that Cowley offered to him. 'Anyway,' he went on. 'I might have been killed. You might have forgotten to load with blanks.'

Doyle laughed nervously, then frowned. He drew his gun and snapped it open, stared at the shells. 'Now *there's* a funny thing . . .'

Cowley shook his head. 'Don't even joke about something like that, you two.' He stared after Rahad. 'He took off like a bat out of hell. Are you sure he'll . . . ?'

He looked round at Bodie, who winked and smiled. 'I'm beginning to know my man. I told him the pay-off place twice. He knows it well. He'll make the delivery to Taylor . . . he has to.'

'We might have scared him off,' said Doyle. 'Shooting, CI5 on the job . . . he might just play safe and forget the whole thing.'

But Cowley disagreed. 'Not him; not Rahad. A very great deal is at stake if Anna Jones speaks out about him, as he thinks she will. He'll take the chance on our enquiry, and he'll still go ahead and set Taylor up.'

The three of them turned and went back to Doyle's car.

Rahad met Taylor in a small park; screened by trees from passing traffic, faces shadowy in the night, Taylor was suspicious, but he shook Rahad's hand.

'Bodie couldn't make it,' Rahad said. 'But I'm the man with the money.'

He passed the case to Taylor who snapped it open, glanced at the money inside and tried to hide his pleasure. He said to Rahad, 'Why are *you* funding this operation?'

'It's personal.' He took a step forward, reached out and took Taylor by the jaw, twisting the youth's face into the light. 'You don't look like much. You don't look tough.'

'I'm the shit-stirrer,' said Taylor. 'The heavies will do their duty. They're good lads.'

'Don't foul up. That's a lot of money, and I don't want to have to take it back . . . the hard way.'

'It'll be okay,' said Taylor, and he hurried away into the darkness.

Bodie had got his Hi-Fi back, and he wasn't happy. Part of the casing was scratched, and those scratches were in obvious places, and Bodie hated damage that could be seen. Infuriatingly, the small print on his ticket did not guarantee to return pawned articles in exactly the same state they had orginally been.

And there was another problem too.

So when Ray Doyle arrived at Bodie's place, and came into the lounge, he was greeted with the sight of Bodie's crouching form, and the sound of Bodie's violently expressed: 'Damn. Damn, damn, damn!'

'Problems?' asked Doyle sweetly.

'I know Cowley,' growled Bodie, not straightening up. 'He won't wear it. I know he won't.'

'Won't wear what?' asked Doyle, looking around, his hands stuffed into the pockets of a wind-cheater.

'I can hear him now. He'll spout some crud about "should have known better, Bodie". He'll deny my expenses for sure.'

Confused, slightly exasperated, Doyle walked over to the equipment, bent down, face close to Bodie's, and whispered,

'Bodie: what the *hell* are you talking about?'

'My Hi-Fi. I went and bought it back.'

'So I see. What about it?'

'Scratched!' Bodie prodded the marks on the casing. '*And* the bugger charged me forty quid more than he gave me for it. Forty quid! "Market's going up" he said. Funny, I said, when I sold it to you the market was going down. "Must be the weather" he said. Forty quid!' He looked at Doyle's grinning face. 'That's all I need, your beaming features.'

Doyle shrugged. 'Well, forty quid. Man's got to make a living.'

'Damn thing's broken, too. My "tweeter's" gone for a Burton!'

'Sounds painful,' Doyle observed, and chuckled at the withering look that Bodie cast towards him. 'But cheer up. Cowley might meet the cost if we pull this one off today.' He glanced at his watch. 'Five hours and three minutes from now.'

Rahad left the Embassy early in the morning, went riding, lunched in Grosvenor Square, spent the afternoon at a sauna, and about five o'clock drove to Johnny Hollis's apartment, to watch the TV special on the demonstration outside his Embassy.

He had heard about the coverage over lunch. It was unusual for a TV station to actually devote a long live broadcast to such a rally, but the issue of Women's Rights for the Middle East was a political hot potato at the moment, and at about midday there was the definite sense of restrained violence in the gathering.

Because of this, the TV crews had been brought in. The sports programmes on each station had run fragmentary coverage of the demonstration, which had caused traffic chaos in Kensington; and the BBC had scheduled a special live programme for five fifteen, the announced time of the major speeches outside the gates of the Embassy.

Rahad would have cleared the Embasssy *anyway* for such a gathering as this. But today he was doubly glad to be clear.

But he wanted to watch. He wanted to see Anna Jones take that small stage, and try and spout her feminist nonsense.

He wanted to see the disturbance that would drag her down into the masses, and crush her underfoot.

Her death would be on TV. It was almost too good to be true.

He was so excited by the prospect that the fact of the coincidence, the way it seemed his every whim was being catered for by the TV station, this fact did not occur to him.

'This is most kind of you, Mister Hollis,' Rahad said as Lucho ushered him into the lounge. 'I thought you might be interested also in seeing how well your ex-man Bodie has done for me. It was a good business deal, Mister Hollis, and I shall hope to deal with you again.'

Hollis, smoking a fat, smelly cigarette, bowed slightly. 'Thank you most kindly. Yes, I'd be very pleased to see Bodie's handiwork. What is it exactly?'

Rahad crossed the room to the wide TV set, and switched it on. 'Do you mind?'

Hollis shrugged. 'You got a horse runing? A dead cert?'

Rahad chuckled. 'A dead cert? Definitely. With the emphasis on *dead*.'

He sat down before the TV, accepted an orange juice from Tina, and waited for the coverage of athletics to be broken, and the cameras to home in on his Embassy, and the crowded, crushed streets outside.

Bodie watched the TV, waiting for Doyle and Cowley to come and fetch him. For the first time in years he didn't mind the interruptions from the coverage of his favourite sport. Each time the cameras showed the demonstration, panning from right to left across an overwhelmingly large sea of faces, Bodie searched hard, felt excited, felt his heart thrill a little at the revelation – for Rahad – that was to come.

The commentator's voice-over was spouting repetitively, the fate of all extended on-the-spot commentaries. 'Crowds have been gathering outside the Embassy since noon, supporters of the growing movement to rescue the women of so many of the Middle Eastern States from what is seen as an unacceptable retreat into servitude. Cultural interference or the Voice of Right, call it what you will, what is most significant about this gathering is that it is supported by members of both sexes, hundreds and thousands of each, men and women from every nation, and every culture, and many of them from the very countries whose religiously fanatical governments are so active in the oppression of women. So far the mood of the demonstrators has been almost genial ... Police reinforcements are, however, standing by in nearby streets ...'

Bodie watched the scenes. In one TV close up shot he saw Taylor, the youth not happy about being filmed and quickly turned away, but not before Bodie had raised his whisky glass to him.

The doorbell rang, and the door opened. Without looking round Bodie said, 'Come in, gents. Just getting a bit of the atmosphere.'

Cowley and Doyle walked up to him, stood one each side of the armchair, watching the screen.

The voice of the TV man said, 'Earlier today Scotland Yard issued a statement affirming that peaceful and reasonable demonstration groups would be allowed to make their views felt ... shortly a petition will be taken to the Embassy and it remains to be seen if anyone at all comes to the door to receive it ...'

Cowley's hand came down on Bodie's shoulder. 'Come on lad. Time to move.'

'Just getting to the best bit,' said Bodie, and Doyle chuckled.

'The best bit's still to come. You don't want to miss that, do you?'

And Bodie drained his glass, picked up his jacket and followed Cowley from the flat.

Rahad was fascinated by it all. The mob outside his Embassy seemed to consist of one, single organism, with thousands of waving, colourful feelers. It was hard to recognise the demonstration as a bunch of individuals. He saw them as part of the same, cancerous growth.

As he watched he fantasised about squashing that mob beneath one, giant foot ... or exploding a bomb in the middle of them.

Hollis watched with indifference, his arm around the girl, Tina, his mind only half on the increasingly outraged mob.

'Any moment now,' said Rahad excitedly. He had not yet seen Anna in the crowds, but had twice glimpsed Taylor, the man who had organised the fracas that was about to break loose.

The commentator was saying, 'Now there seems to be some disturbance at the back of the crowd . . . a group trying to force its way through . . . '

'Yes . . . ' breathed Rahad, leaning forward in his seat, eyes glued to the set. He could see the great body of the mob rippling, distorting as Taylor's men went into action, or as some local disturbance set up eddy currents of people.

'The police hopes for a "peaceful and reasonable" demonstration . . . ' said the TV man, ' . . . appear to be threatened by the will of the mob . . . and yes, that is the only word to describe the scene here of the last few minutes . . . a mass of people rapidly becoming a mob . . . '

Rahad waved his glass happily at Tina, who giggled and stood up to refill the vessel with orange juice. Rahad smiled at her, satisfaction making him glow.

'There is definitely a militant group making its weight felt now . . . its considerable weight . . . forcing its way through . . . escorting someone . . . '

Rahad watched intently. His hands had begun to shake a little. He was witnessing a certain death, not a play, not a film, but the actual moment of someone's killing, and it was unusual for him to be watching and not doing. He found himself enthralled . . . excited!

On the TV, fighting had broken out. The commentator's voice was rising in pitch. 'Yes, it's the anti-Arab group coming to the fore now . . . they're commanding the stage . . . and coming through is Anna Jones, daughter of Dame Sarah Jones, herself so voluble against the Muslim cause . . . and there she is now, Anna Jones, moving up to the steps, no doubt to try and make a speech . . . '

Rahad's breath caught in his throat, but then he managed to shout, 'Kill her! Why don't they kill her?'

Hollis exchanged a look with Hart, then grinned, and stared at the TV screen. Rahad's heart was going thunderously. He could see the blonde girl being bustled through the crowds, but instead of being knocked down, she was actually thrust through the crushing masses, almost ejected onto the stage, where she steadied herself, stood upright, and raised her hands to the mob!

Tall, blonde, slim ... the bespectacled girl certainly had presence, and she waved for silence, Taylor standing by her, his arms raised also.

Rahad screeched with frustration and fury. He crossed the room to the screen, dropped to his knees and stared at Anna.

But it wasn't Anna! This woman wasn't the lovely Anna Jones who had shared his bed, and almost his heart! This girl was plain, sour-faced. She had no class.

This wasn't Anna!

And with a sudden, sickening, deafening realisation, his head filled with the noise of the baying crowds, his eyes dizzy with the blur of the screen, and the gaudy colours of the room, Tefali Rahad realised that he had been taken, well and truly taken ...

He had fallen into a trap.

He had played straight into the hands of George Cowley!

Cowley kicked open the door of the apartment. He had heard Rahad's cry of frustrated rage, and all three of the CI5 men had broken into spontaneous, delighted grins.

'I'd love to have seen his face,' said Bodie.

'No shooting,' said Cowley, and Bodie put his gun away.

'But you don't mind a bit of bashing, do you sir?' That from Doyle. Cowley's answer: a foot raised, a foot slammed hard against the door to Hollis's suite of rooms.

An unlikely wild bunch, Cowley, Doyle and Bodie moved fast and heavy into the room.

Lucho lurched away from his position by the door. He had been watching Rahad's exhibition in something akin to bemusement, and he had not heard the whispering outside the door. He tried to grab Doyle, but Doyle ducked under the fists and slammed the man hard, with two hands, in the stomach. As Lucho doubled up, winded. Doyle's knee jerked up and then his foot.

'He was mine,' said Bodie petulantly, then turned as Hart came for him, catching him a glancing blow on the side of the head. Bodie moved fluently on his feet, chopped at Hart, making him stagger, then punched him — three times. He didn't get up.

Doyle said, 'Now *he* was yours.'

Then he and Bodie followed George Cowley to the TV lounge, where Johnny Hollis was backed up against a wall, toupee askew, face sweating, no sign of Tina for a comforting reassuring grope.

Rahad stood by the TV, face red, eyes ablaze with fury. Doyle's hand rested on his gun, waiting for the slightest movement of Rahad's hands towards any concealed pistol.

Hollis stammered, 'I want a lawyer.'

Bodie, vengefully, walked over and clipped him brutally in the mouth. 'Another word out of you and what you'll want is a dentist and a plastic surgeon.' Hollis nodded vigorously, understanding Bodie well. Bodie flexed his hand, the cut having reopened during his short dance with Martin Hart.

Doyle began to close in on Tefali Rahad, but Cowley called him back.

Calmly, acting with the utmost correctness, Cowley said, 'Mister Rahad has diplomatic immunity, is that not right, Mister Rahad?'

Falteringly, Rahad said, 'That is correct. Yes. And why have you broken in here?'

'Broken in? Mister Hollis invited us, isn't that right?' As he spoke, Cowley glanced at Bodie who nudged Johnny Hollis in the ribs, causing Hollis to groan, and nod. Bodie said, 'Mister Hollis says, yes, that's quite correct.'

George Cowley walked up to Rahad, looked him straight in the eye, then smiled. 'We respect your diplomatic immunity, sir. In fact, the relationship between our country and your . . . "beloved leader" is such that we feel compelled to show him these.'

He reached into his coat pocket and drew out a pack of photographs. Rahad took them, flicked through them. He couldn't resist a wry little smile.

He was looking at grainy, infra-red photographs of he and Taylor exchanging the money in the park; Taylor had briefly shaken hands with him as he had arrived, and that moment had been captured too.

Cowley said, 'The man is ... but then, you know him, Mister Rahad. Harry Taylor is a prime mover in Anna Jones's political group, a group dedicated to the overthrow of your President. And there you are, Mister Rahad, in cahoots. Giving him money. The photograph could have been faked, of course, but the fact that you urgently changed an amount of sterling pounds into Swiss francs ... that is a matter of record.' He smiled at Rahad. 'You even had to make a special arrangement outside banking hours.'

Rahad handed back the photographs, looked at Bodie, who gave him a thin smile. Cowley said, 'I really have enjoyed this little game, Mister Rahad. But you really aren't a very good player.'

Rahad bowed. 'And the girl Anna, I suppose she was ... '

Cowley merely said, 'Very expensive.'

'I have been tricked. Set up. I shall have no hesitation in saying so.'

'By all means,' said Cowley smugly. 'But that will be a matter for your President to decide. And the way your regime is at the moment ... it feeds on doubts and suspicions. Do you know what I think? I think your President will regard this as a friendly act, a concern for his safety. I think it will strengthen the relationship between our countries. I think,' he finished, most deliberately, 'I think you will be recalled, and our country will be rid of a murderer and an assassin.'

Rahad said, almost plaintively, 'You will be killing me.'

'Us, Mister Rahad? Our hands will be bloodless. Any killing will be done by your own countrymen ... a sword, I believe, against a neatly exposed neck? Good day, Mister Rahad. Oh, by the way. There's a police car downstairs, waiting to escort you back to your Embassy.'

He turned and walked from the room, Doyle following. Bodie grinned at Hollis, nudged him once more in the ribs, and said, 'Ciao!'

As he walked from the flat the girl Tina, holding a small suitcase, rushed out after him, smiling at him as they waited by the lift.

'He wears a toupee too, you know,' said Doyle slyly.

Epilogue

Ray Doyle looked more groomed than he had done for a month, hair trimmed and actually brushed, lithe, athletic body decked out in natty clothes. His flat, too, was tidy, to a degree that astonished Bodie as he arrived for the informal evening to celebrate Rahad's demise.

Bodie whistled admiringly, first at Doyle, then at the apartment, with its corner lights, and little trays of cocktail tasties on the table.

'Make no comments,' said Doyle.

'I didn't say a thing,' said Bodie, and grinned. 'May I have a nut?'

'Help yourself. Just leave some for the others.'

Bodie grabbed a handful of cashews and chewed slowly, watching as Doyle fussed around, one eye on his handiwork, the other on Bodie, whom he did not trust. Bodie asked, 'Hooked, are you?'

'I warned you . . . no cracks!'

'On a hooker. That must be where the name . . . ' he broke off as a gherkin flew across the room, narrowly missing him.

'Pick that up!' said Doyle, and Bodie, chuckling, stooped to obey.

'This is really formal,' he said, dumping the dirtied vegetable in a waste bin.

'I mean it to be.'

'One question.' Bodie shovelled nuts into his mouth. 'Her presence here . . . will the department have to pay for . . . '

Doyle picked up a bottle, looked evil, looked mad: 'I warned you!'

'All right, all right.'

But the moods were too good for any mischievous aside to spoil an evening. Rahad had been recalled home almost immediately, and Cowley was certain that within hours of his touching down at the largest International Airport of his homeland, his head and his body would be rolling in different directions.

The game had been won, and CI5 had not fired a shot in anger. Just blanks.

The door buzzer went. 'Get that, will you?' said Doyle, and as Bodie moved across the room, Doyle eased the cork out of a bottle of iced champagne. The cork popped satisfyingly.

Cowley entered the apartment, looking pleased as punch, and slightly flushed. He'd been at the whisky, and was clearly having a good time.

On his arm, looking equally pleased with herself, was Anna. Not the feminist, anti-Arab, Rights for Muslim Women, political animal Anna Jones ... not the *real* Anna Jones. She was probably still running-off political pamphlets in some cat-littered attic in Shepherds Bush, oblivious to her unwitting involvement in Operation Fix Rahad. Taylor had been instructed to say nothing, and appeared to have obeyed that instruction, even though he was Anna Jones's right hand man. Money had acquired his silence.

No, this Anna was the beautiful woman who had beguiled Tefali Rahad, and she greeted Doyle with a wink and a charming smile.

Cowley said, 'Good evening Doyle ... Bodie ... We've been talking about old times.'

Bodie almost choked on a nut, the line sounding more euphemistic, even, than 'looking at my etchings'. 'Old times sir?'

Cowley scowled at him, Anna looking knowing and amused. 'Calm yourself, Bodie. Yes, old times. It transpires that I knew. . . . Anna's ... ' he smiled at her, 'Anna's father very well.'

'In the bad old corrupt days,' said Anna. 'Daddy was a stockbroker. Mm, champagne.'

Doyle had produced a tray with bubbling glasses upon it. Cowley said, 'What shall we drink to?'

'Tefali Rahad, who's become his own pain in the neck?' That suggestion was from Bodie, and George Cowley disapproved strongly. 'Och no, lad. That would leave a sour taste.'

Ray Doyle with a charming smile and a flash of his angelic blue eyes, said, 'Let's drink to a very special lady. Anna. . . ' He raised his glass.

Cowley: 'Aye, that'll do fine. To Anna.'

Bodie smirked obviously, raised his glass to his lips. 'I'll drink to that.'

Anna looked from each to the other, then raised her glass before her. 'A lady,' she echoed. 'A very special lady. Yes, I like that. I'm very definitely that. If I weren't . . . ' she winked at Doyle again. 'I'd be out of business!'

TRAVERSE OF THE GODS

by Bob Langley

The Eiger, 1944 – In a desperate attempt to turn defeat into victory, German and American mountaineers are locked in an appalling struggle on the notorious North Wall of Europe's deadliest mountain – a struggle with vital implications for the development of the atomic bomb.

'Brilliant . . . in a class by itself'
Jack Higgins

'Written in the best adventure tradition'
Publishers Weekly

ADVENTURE/THRILLER   0 7221 5410 0   £1.50

And don't miss Bob Langley's other exciting thrillers:
DEATH STALK
WAR OF THE RUNNING FOX
WARLORDS
– also available in Sphere Books